ONE
HELL OF A
LOVER

ONE
HELL OF A
LOVER

UNNI R.

Translated from the Malayalam by J. Devika

VINTAGE
An imprint of Penguin Random House

VINTAGE

USA | Canada | UK | Ireland | Australia
New Zealand | India | South Africa | China

Vintage is part of the Penguin Random House group of companies
whose addresses can be found at global.penguinrandomhouse.com

Published by Penguin Random House India Pvt. Ltd
4th Floor, Capital Tower 1, MG Road,
Gurugram 122 002, Haryana, India

Penguin
Random House
India

First published in English by Eka, an imprint of Westland Publications
Private Limited in 2019
Published in Vintage by Penguin Random House India 2022

Copyright © Unni R. 2019
Translation copyright © J. Devika. 2019
Illustrations: Elwin Charly

10 9 8 7 6 5 4 3 2 1

ISBN 9780670097463

Typeset by Jojy Philip, New Delhi 110015
Printed at Thomson Press India Ltd, New Delhi

www.penguin.co.in

To my mother, wife and daughter—
the three women who have stood by me at a time when
writers are killed for writing.

Contents

'Asle has a sister almost as old as he is. He always holds his sister's hand. And a big boy tells Asle that he always holds girls hands, always.'

—'Girls', *Scenes from a Childhood* by Jon Fosse

One Hell of a Lover

1

'Lover: the man of endless longing, ceaseless lust'—Matha Mappila. The only thing people aren't really sure about is his age—eighty or ninety. About other stuff, dead sure they are. Even today, he lifts daily on his dick a five-kilo block of cold iron. Once a year, every year, deflowers three virgins on the same day. Works out every day at the crack of dawn. Downs thirty native-hens' eggs whipped with saffron. Needs a woman carnally, all the time. It is this fearsome man who has sent word, asking to meet urgently.

Too much drink, strange dreams and mixed-up talk—these three had conspired to keep me under house arrest for one whole year. My friend Sasankan claims that I looked at the weights and scales in Thanka chechi's corner shop and said that they were like a Picasso sculpture. I did not believe him. But when he, who had dropped out of school in Class 4 and knew nothing but the carpenter's craft, mentioned Van Gogh, I began to doubt myself. The SNDP Sakha office was being painted a bright yellow, and I apparently told the secretary that the Sakha office in Amsterdam was bright yellow, thanks to a painter called Van Gogh. And not just that—the cuss-words that rained down on me when I tried a Duchamp by drawing moustaches on the hairless faces of Siva and Krishna in the Sivakashi calendar that hung in the local barber's shop, justified my self-doubt all the more. Still, I had not completely stopped believing in myself. But the day Kottayil Sankara Pillai Saar came to see me, I regretted having disregarded Sasankan.

He came to our house early in the morning. I was just waking up. He had taught us—Padmini and me—maths at school. The old regard still lingered. She too, like me, must have wondered why he had dropped in so early in the day.

'Where is Parameswaran?' he asked.

'Not yet up,' Padmini replied respectfully, gently pushing a chair forward so that he could sit.

Before he sat down, Saar said, 'Good!'

Though I didn't see what was good about me not being up in the morning, I lay in bed, listening closely through the gap in the door.

'Well, please don't feel bad,' he began in his unassuming way. 'Yesterday, I had called Parameswaran to help mend my window.'

Though I wanted to declare loudly, right from where I lay, that I had, in truth, no memory at all of meeting him, the feeling that he, an elderly person, that too my teacher, would not utter a blatant lie made me want to keep listening.

'Do you know what Parameswaran said to that?'

Whipping up anxiety needlessly is an old habit of his, from classroom days of old. A surge of worry made me leap up from the mat quite unknowingly.

'He said, let's get Kanayi Kunhiraman to repair it.'

I nearly called aloud to God Almighty, but suppressing the urge, looked at Padmini. Her face was blank as she kept looking at Saar. She probably thought that this Kunhiraman was some senior carpenter, or maybe some distant uncle of my father's—that's why she was so still, I realised. And that's probably why Saar delivered a short introduction on Kanayi. After the short lesson, seeing Padmini's flushed face turn decisively towards the left, where my room is, he added, 'I would say, take good care of him.'

There was no reason to disbelieve Saar. But my problem was whether I'd say such a thing. Kanayi was my teacher. A sculptor I respected. At the interview for admission to the Fine Arts College, I was asked to name three of my favourite sculptors, and his name was in the list I had made, along with Ramkinkar and Roy Choudhury, without knowing that he was seated in front of me.

After Sankara Pillai Saar left, all that Padmini said to me was this: 'Take a bath, get ready. We are going to the doctor.'

I did not object. The doctor was a man with chubby cheeks. I hugged him and renewed our friendship.

'Mr Francis Bacon, long time!' I said.

When he and Padmini threw surprised looks at me, I told them about our connection.

'I saw Francis Bacon for the first time when I was a student at the Fine Arts College,' I told Padmini. Turning to the doctor, I asked, 'Remember, Mr Bacon?'

He immediately shook his head in agreement—probably because he was an affable person—and said, 'Of course, of course I do, what a question!' And since he too possessed the shrewdness of all intelligent doctors, he cleverly extracted from me the history of my meeting with Francis Bacon.

I was in my third year in Sculpture at the Fine Arts College then. I was coming out of Mukkadan's Bar and walking through Palayam Market. That was two days after I'd seen Bacon's portrait by Lucian Freud in my teacher Nandakumar's personal collection. Bacon was standing right next to the mud-filled, horribly stinky abattoir inside the market. I greeted him familiarly. There was some reluctance to respond, but I told him anyway, 'The way your Pope Innocent screams would give even Velazquez the jitters!' This single sentence put him at ease, and he held out his hand. The fact that Celia Paul, one of Lucian Freud's lovers, was born in Thiruvananthapuram, was news to him. He graciously tolerated some stupid things that I spewed unabashedly, the brash youth that I was. When I let him know that I was a student of sculpture and that Giacometti was my favourite, he said that he preferred Giacometti's sketches to his sculptures.

I discreetly let George, a painting student and friend, know about my encounter with Francis Bacon. He had no talent for keeping secrets, and soon, the whole college knew. One night, A.C.K. Raja came to my hostel room along with George. He spoke for some time about painting, and handed me some money, suggesting that I go home, rest awhile, and return after. George came with me the next day. I gave him a hint about how some members of the Radical Painters' group were envious of my meeting with Francis Bacon at Palayam. 'Don't bother about all that'—that was his advice.

Waking up early in the morning, rubbing scented kaiyyonni oil generously on my head, bathing in the river, eating Amma's delicious food, walking with Padmini on her way back from the typing class through the lane near the temple till her house—my life was rolling on, peacefully, until the SNDP Sakha people asked if I could make a life-size statue of Sree Narayana Guru for them. That was a chance to prove myself as a sculptor, and I didn't let it go.

On the condition that they provided me with good money, good food and good liquor, I took up the job. All three were made available in plenty. But as it progressed, every mouthful of arrack brought up the question whether the liberators were actually imprisoned in their own statues. It was around then, while walking home one night, that I ran into the Guru. Right under the mango tree where I used to wait for Padmini! I didn't recognize him at first. The man looked totally different from all his images and statues. Long legs, like a Giacometti sculpture! A face with grand lines and furrows, like Ramkinkar's bust of Tagore!

'You are in confusion, aren't you, Parameswaran?' the Guru asked.

He said 'confusion' in English. How come he spoke English? I doubted for a moment. So my response was a counter-question.

'Guru, why didn't you speak to Gandhi in English?'

He smiled as he replied, 'Gandhi's English pronunciation is stuffed with Englishmen.'

The lane wanted us to walk together; it shed its narrowness and grew expansive.

'What do I need a shrine or statue for?' he asked.

I did not reply. He pulled out two of his declarations from the waist-fold of his mundu—the one which said that temples were not to be encouraged anymore, and the one from *Prabuddha Keralam*, which said that he had no caste. I read both and looked at him.

'I hope you have no more doubts.'

I laughed and hugged him.

'This is the first time a drunk has touched me,' he said, turning somewhat solemn.

To dodge the discomfort, I said diffidently, 'What do I do, am I not an artist?'

Walking away into the dark on his long legs, the Guru responded, 'Better than Gangajal.'

Two weeks later, the statue was ready. The Ezhava grandees and the Sakha members looked at it only once. Their eyes were then directed at me. I handed them the two messages the Guru had made me read. Somebody picked up a long stick. The head shattered and the life-size statue joined the earth, attaining the ultimate release.

That very afternoon, I was taken to Dr Basheer's hospital. Later, a relative told me that on the way there, I kept mumbling throughout that I was not born to be a sculptor, I was not born even to live, that I wasn't born for anything.

When I returned to college after Dr Basheer's treatment, there was a letter waiting for me. 'Friend,' it said, 'I am sorry that I could not see the face of your statue of the Guru.' It was signed by Matha Mappila. That letter puzzled me not a little. Matha Mappila, who had shaken by their very roots the days of my youth, had sent me a letter! From then on, whenever I came home for the holidays, I tried to meet him. But all my efforts inevitably failed. As the years went by, I gave up. So this desire that I had let loose into the wastelands of forgetfulness had now been summoned up by his emissary.

'Taking him along is fine,' said Padmini, 'but don't you dare give him a drop of liquor!'

'Yes, no liquor,' he promised her.

'Satan-worship won't work with me,' Padmini made doubly sure.

The man looked at me. I shook my head, meaning yes.

2

The path that went to Matha Mappila's house was like a riddle. No one trod it. The house stood in the middle of a twenty-five-acre plot. It could not be seen from the outside because of the dense trees growing all around. The compound wall was the height of two full-grown men, and was lined with sharp spikes of iron. In that secluded spot, the only other structure was a church, which stood directly opposite Matha Mappila's property. It was used only two times a year, that church. The worshippers who went there on those two days were more into sharing stories about what went on inside those walls and figuring out ways to manage a peep inside. Their only solace lay in the report from the fellows who climbed atop the tall tamarind tree in the churchyard around Christmas to put up the Christmas stars and set the microphone. They said that everyone there went around buck naked, that young girls without a stitch on their bodies watered the plants, and that Matha Mappila strew rice grains on his erect dick and got doves to feed on them.

The priest knew well that even during Mass, the believers were busy whispering amongst themselves about that unbelieving son of Satan, Matha Mappila. And so he never failed to put before them, as an example of a sinner, the tale of a man who had lived a long time ago in Goa, a man of impure birth. Everyone knew that Matha was the sinner born to a Catholic girl with that white devil from Goa.

In the last homily, the priest told them that Matha worshipped Satan and had had to flee Goa after sacrificing a virgin.

Sitting in the backseat of the old Mark II Ambassador car, I asked Matha's emissary, 'Does he really worship Satan?'

He was totally focused on driving and so my question lingered for some time at his ear-step, and then, disappointed, it rolled down the car's window, fell out, and disappeared into the world.

When the car reached the massive gates, the eerie shadows that hung upside down in the trees inside the compound came over to check. The rusty gates said something raspingly as they swung open. No sooner had we entered than they swung right back, muttering the same vague and grating words. A couple of huge pigs came hurtling across the path. On their curly little tails, big butterflies rode, their wings flung wide open. The shrubbery was green and dense on both sides of the path, and as we passed, a million tongues, bluish and forked, leapt out of it to lick the car's ferrous body. The car's wheels struck the gnarled tree-roots which lay on the path like intestines ripped out of a corpse; it juddered and swerved. I felt fear crouching in me; I could hear its muffled footsteps. It was all of a sudden then, that a cloud of *vettu-kili*—locusts, birds, locust-birds—emerged from the thick foliage and barred our way like a troop of soldiers. The driver stopped the car. I could hear the sounds of a visual language that the birds wrote with their beaks. The writing done, they regrouped ahead of and behind the car. Escorting us till the door of a two-storeyed mansion, they disappeared into the thickets.

The more my eyes struggled to get a sense of the proportions of that house, the more it grew. The more you looked at the high ceiling, the higher it rose. A huge chandelier, shaped like an eye, hung from it. On the walls hung a massive collection of feathers of all kinds. The silence of the staircase winding towards the upper floor was unnerving. I searched for the man who had brought me here. He was nowhere to be seen. As I shut my eyes with a long sigh, I heard footsteps descending the stairs. When I opened my eyes, I saw a short man, his back hunched a bit. Under his mundu, which fell to his knees, the tail-end of his loincloth could be seen; it looked like a pig-tail. I made respectful sounds. In response, he gestured to me to sit down.

Sitting on a stool across from me, he said, 'It was he who called you, not me.'

This hunchback was not Matha Mappila, it was clear. Besides, from all the stories through which Matha

Mappila's image had grown and grown, he was at least seven feet tall and endowed with beefy muscles to match.

'I've been instructed to tell you something.'

I tried to suppress the eagerness to hear, but could not. Therefore an ugly croak, sounding like a fart, rose up from the depths of my throat.

'You have to make a sculpture,' said the hunchbacked man.

That left me shivering in my chair, and I looked at his face again, not believing my ears. No change showed on his face. His words were short, like his body; so too were his expressions.

'There will be no dearth of money.'

I heard that bit about cash in the middle of a struggle to keep myself from falling off the chair. Knowing well that my reins were too weak to hold back the joy that was now mounted on a thousand steeds, I leaned my head on the back of the chair. He sensed that I was in no shape to hear anything more, and it was probably because of that that he allowed us a short interval before he continued.

'The sculpture you have to make is the Pieta. To be placed in front of the church.'

Pieta? Commissioned by a Satan-worshipper? My tongue was paralysed as the doubts that tore through my mind formed a net and dragged me down. He completed the commissioning during my silence.

'Mary's hands are not to bear Christ.'

Who then—the words needed to ask that question leapt up to my mouth, but failed to emerge as sound and phrase.

'Mary's face shouldn't be Mary's.'

Unexpected blows to the body of an already fully-drained man can eclipse his mind. I realised later that all that the man in such a condition says emerges usually from a state of semi-consciousness.

'The face should be that of Chungam Kuttyamma. And no clothes. She must be nude.'

When I returned to consciousness, the hunchbacked man was holding out money.

'Here's two lakh rupees … If you don't mind, let us begin work tomorrow itself.'

Stripping the Pieta naked. A denial of history for sure. But before guilt could assail me, my hands had accepted the money.

'I need two days' time,' I somehow scrambled for the words and found them.

The hunchback agreed.

'The car will come to pick you up after two days.'

Before I got up to leave, seizing the little courage I could muster, I asked, 'Can I … see …'

'Not today.'

3

'He's crazier than Achan. Or else why would he spend so much on a statue?' I heard my daughter ask Padmini.

Padmini, however, was simply not able to get over the thrill of counting the money.

I opened my old suitcase. It opened reluctantly, hanging back briefly before stretching itself open. It clearly nursed a gripe about not being opened in a long time. I had shut everything inside the box when I realised that after finishing at Fine Arts College, the only work a sculptor could find was of a drawing-master in a school. The book *Art Criticism: Marxist Norms* was moth-eaten but largely unharmed. The moths most probably lost some teeth trying to chew it and so left it alone. Some movie-screening flyers of the Chithralekha Film Society, the detailed brochure of the Radical Painters' camp at Alappad, Edasseri's poems, old sketchbooks—the book about Michelangelo at the bottom of the suitcase was thick enough to take the weight of all these in the darkness inside it. Idiotic librarians had stamped the college's round seal—out of sheer vengeance almost—on the colour plates of Michelangelo's statues and sketches. Sitting in the teashop outside the college with this very book open on my lap, I had once asked Radhamani, who was a student of Applied Arts, why Mary, who held the body of Christ lowered from the cross, looked so young. Her reply was quick and sharp like a slap.

'Because she gave birth while still a virgin.'

From that reply began long debates about the beauty of women who never gave birth, lasting many nights after.

'Hey, the news that Matha Mappila has summoned you has spread all over,' Padmini's forthright voice dragged me back mercilessly into the present.

I put the memories and Michelangelo back into the darkness of the suitcase.

'And listen—don't tell anyone why you were called there, no matter who asks.' The voice came from the kitchen, and Padmini came along with it, holding the pot-handler-rag.

'What's wrong in saying openly that one's sculpting a statue?'

'Don't let people wag their tongues—about your sculpture-vulture-art-fart, okay? This family doesn't starve because someone else in this house is slaving away all day.'

I knew that she wouldn't calm down, even though our daughter came and held her hands. So I stepped out. It would take till night for her to cool down.

'Ssh ... ssh ...'

It was Sasankan, behind the pathal plants, clicking his tongue like some lizard on a wall. What is it, I asked with a shake of my head. He gestured, asking me to come to the pond behind the house.

'Is it true?'

He sounded like he would collapse from sheer curiosity.

'Yes.'

'Did you see him?'

His limbs were quivering. His tongue darted out to wet his lips and bring them back to life.

'I saw him.'

'And?'

'Seven feet tall. And with muscles to match.'

Sasankan called out to his Maker and sank into the wet mud beside the pond. Because I knew well what had made his legs go weak, I too sat down near him.

'Not a trace of age on his face. A real stud. And ...'

'And ...?'

'Naked, completely naked.'

That naked body, that masculinity untouched by age, they drowned Sasankan in darkness for some time. When he rose up again, his words had dried up. He heard the rest balancing himself on the tip of a single breath.

'When I reached his house, two naked girls opened the door. They must have been seventeen or eighteen. They took my hand and led me to a big chair. They fed me sweetmeats, offered me a large tumbler of milk, and perfumed my body with the sweet smoke of frankincense. As I wafted dreamily in that delectable cloud of aroma, Matha Mappila entered, with four naked women by his side. I was stunned, rooted to the spot, unable even to rise from the chair. He came up and said just one thing: Make me a statue.' My narration ended there. I waited for Sasankan to return to space and time.

In the end, secure in his return, Sasankan asked,

'Whose statue?'

My face contorted that moment into a dramatic grin. When it was evident that his curiosity would fall off its stalk any moment, I revealed, 'Of Chungam Kuttyamma.'

In that moment, I saw in his eyes the Sasankan of old times. And Sasankan saw the Parameswaran of old. We came of age during the Emergency. Aniyan chettan was a man who could not do without a bit of politics in everything, even in frothing up the tea or making a dosa. That man gave up politics after the Emergency was declared. And it was in such a mood that he told us about Chungam Kuttyamma as though it were a great secret.

'In the big house near the Panchayat office, a nice piece from Chungam has come to stay. Kuttyamma, that's her name. They say that Sheela and Jayabharathy of the movies would die of shame in front of her!'

Jayabharathy's sensuous swaying in the song about adorning her face with a spot of kumkum, from the movie *Guruvayoor Kesavan*, was at this time shoving us into a state of giddy arousal. And then, on top of it, came Aniyan chettan's description.

'Big cinema people and businessmen are coming and going daily!'

Cursing out of sheer envy that the Emergency did not seem to have had an impact on such agencies, we listened to the rest of Aniyan chettan's report.

'On some nights, there's a trip in an Impala car. With the windows covered so you can't see anything.'

Standing outside the sky-high wall near the Panchayat office, we let loose our senses on many a day, trying to capture the unseen beauty behind it through fragrance or music. When it all failed, we invoked it all into our fists. At the end of the invocation, we let free white cranes into the deep throat of the toilet-pot.

'Parameswara ...'

I turned to Sasankan. His voice was wan, like his face.

'Where is the lady now?'

I too hung at the other end of his anxious query. That secret too was revealed to us one day by the teashop-man, Aniyan chettan.

'Now others are not coming. Just one.'

Something froze inside us.

'One Matha Mappila. He's bought the estate near the church on the hill. He's supposed to be a real lady-killer. He can make a woman have an orgasm by just looking at her—that's what they say.'

Sasankan gripped my shoulder hard. 'Fucking pig!' we swore instantly.

When the Emergency ended and Aniyan chettan went back to talking politics again, new storytellers took the stage. Their stories were full of the sort of wind and spray that could sweep away our minds in a trice. The main character was a Mappila man from Thalassery. He delivered provisions to Kuttyamma's household every month. In the beginning, he used to leave them at the doorstep and the Nepalese servant-girls would take them in. They were not allowed to speak with anyone outside. Once, the man left a note in a packet of sweets that had come from some foreign place, asking to meet. Kuttyamma did not turn him down. But she let him see only her body from below the neck. Then it became a regular thing, and the Mappila would reduce his prices in return for the sight of her body. But soon he grew tired of seeing the same thing over and over again, and requested her to show her face once. She said she would lift her veil if he fulfilled a task. He agreed. 'Curl a viper on your cock,' she said. The man fainted, and never returned. It was around this time that Matha Mappila entered Kuttyamma's life. When she said that he was indeed one hell of a lover, he took her on his neck, strong as that of an ox, and leapt over the high wall of the house. That's what people here still say about him: *The* Lover, Man of Ceaseless Lust.

4

The main impediment to my work was that there was no photo of Kuttyamma available. Whenever I mentioned this to the hunchback, he would ask me to wait and assure me that Matha Mappila would find a way. On all such occasions, I would also disclose obliquely my desire to meet Matha Mappila, and the response would invariably be: Wait, it is not yet time.

Though I was willing to wait, it was impossible to control my curiosity, and so I parted the thatch in my workshed to make a gap. Through the gap, the long windows on the second floor of Matha Mappila's mansion were visible. If they were opened at some point, one might catch a glimpse of at least his shadow. But the only thing I saw daily was a short, dark man run around outside the house, carrying on his neck a massive bull. As he ran, a cock—its legs chained—would fly out of the house and swipe its beak at the bull. The dark legs would falter only for a second when the bull roared in pain as the beak tore into its flesh. When the bull's blood mingled with its sweat and dripped onto the ground, hordes of pigs would descend squealing to lick it. The butterflies on their tails would rise and fall in the air synchronously, writing a language unique to them.

5

Padmini was relieved that I was finally going to start some proper, regular work. Till now, I hadn't told her what I was going to make, or that I still hadn't begun the task. She wasn't interested in the least. The local folk were curious, though. But Padmini made sure their inquiries did not cross our doorstep.

Only once, when the local priest came to our house along with Sasankan, did she stay quiet in the face of such interference.

'I hope you won't take offense at what I am about to say,' he asked, sipping the sweet coffee Padmini had handed him.

'Tell me, Father,' I answered courteously.

'Though we belong to different faiths, shouldn't we agree on some things?'

I couldn't see what he meant. Christ used to speak in metaphors. But this wasn't that.

'You know that this Matha Mappila is an unbeliever and someone who does vile things. I heard that you're going to make some new-fangled statue for him?'

I nodded my head in agreement.

'Near his wall means in front of our church, you know that, right?'

I nodded again.

'Is that a wrong thing, Parameswara?'

I didn't bother to ask: What's so wrong about that? Instead, in a low voice that sounded humble beyond compare, I said, 'It isn't what you think, Father. He's erecting a Pieta there.'

I saw Sasankan's gaze turn swiftly to me; I ducked it and trained all my attention on the priest. Not able to believe my words, the priest looked at me for a moment, stupefied, and asked, 'Pieta?'

'Yes.'

'No matter how lost, all sinners will receive a revelation from God sometime,' he said that to no one in particular and fell silent. Then, feeling relieved, he drank up the coffee and prepared to leave. Sasankan and I went with him to the gate.

'May the Lord bless you!' he said before he stepped out.

Like two sinners, we nodded our heads.

6

I heard a brief description of Chungam Kuttyamma's face and body from the hunchbacked man. Matha Mappila wanted sketches to be prepared using those details, he said. I was amazed at how much more beautiful this image was compared with the one that lit up the jerking-off hours in my teenage.

I translated that description into ten sketches. The hunchback would return with detailed comments and suggestions from Matha Mappila. One day he said, 'Alright. Let us begin now.'

In the end, the mystery that never lifted its veil to any of us, the sheer gumption that asked in return for a glimpse of its face, a viper coiled on an erect cock—that mysterious face was born at my fingertips. As I gazed at the beauty that Matha Mappila now meant to return to us, Lot—the incestuous father of two daughters who had failed them at the Fall of Sodom in the Bible—turned into the fourth face of Lord Brahma. The dead weight of the heads of Fathers who had led us astray began to throw me into disarray. From now till its completion, there would be no Kutty-Amma—only Kutty, my child whom I was carving; my own daughter-woman. And there was also the irony that the moment it was complete, the 'Kutty' would become 'Amma'. How meaningful the name— Kutty-Amma. Dearest One, who enthralled my youth, did you know how many Oceans of Milk you churned beneath my waist?

'There's something else to be done,' the hunchback's voice made me shake off the memory of my ecstasy and turn towards him somewhat fearfully.

'The body should have sixty-four birthmarks.'

That this number sounded odd to me must have shown on my face, and so he clarified: 'They stand for the sixty-four arts.'

He gave me a note that specified where each of the moles—'arts'—were to be placed. Starting from inside the left ear-lobe, ending below the little toe on the right foot—the sixty-four arts!

7

They say that Matha Mappila and Kuttyamma would lie together completely naked in the dark and make love with words. It was he who taught her that words are swifter, more agile and free-flowing than the body. He believed that the sixty-fifth art was the art of silence. In the experiments around this art, he made Kuttyamma stand naked in the moonlight. The local pundits say of her death-in-sex that after eleven carnal unions, during the twelfth, the universe fell silent and her life-force rose up in the moonlight through the vagina.

Sasankan looked up at the full moon.

'He sure is from hell, isn't he?'

I said nothing. I was looking up too, but my eyes were fixed on the sky on which semen had collected to form a high roof.

I told him: 'I saw her.'

He grabbed my shoulders and asked, 'Really?'

I nodded.

'So she isn't dead?'

From within the unexplainable biological complication that I fell into when my fingers became a uterus of sorts, I replied, 'No.'

8

After the casting in cement was done and lunch was over, I was idling, when a horde of pigs with butterflies on their tails sauntered up to me. Before I could move away, they surrounded me. The butterflies, rising and falling on pig-tails, asked me:

'How many girls have you fucked at the same time?'

'Just one.'

The pigs broke into derisive giggles.

'How many have you kissed?'

That was a she-pig, from the back.

'Two. Or two and a half.'

'What's the two and a half?' A red butterfly wanted to know.

'Two of them were my lovers. The third, I tried to kiss in the crowd at the temple fair. But the kiss fell on the sleeve of her blouse.'

They laughed again. Then, the smallest, blind, and perhaps the oldest of the pigs pushed aside the others and stood before me. Its face made me fearful, truly.

'You are in love with this sculpture, aren't you?'

Before the question was completed, a pack of bandicoots and black cats, and the cock shaking its long chains, surrounded me. My heart sounded like it were digging a deep pit.

'Tell us nothing but the truth,' the blind pig ordered.

When I leapt up, repeating 'no, no,' a very ordinary day was dawning outside the window.

9

Because I did not want even the sunlight to peep in, I had patched up the gap in the thatched wall. And I locked the shed every night after work, with the hunchback's permission and kept the key; I did not want any intrusion.

'He will come here only after it is ready,' the hunchback had said.

In a few days, the statue would be cast. Then the scales of plaster covering its body would be scraped off. The figure that emerged would have to be bathed and baptized with water, like a newborn.

10

Though Sasankan turned up after dinner one night, with his big ears and endless envy to hear stories of Matha Mappila, I did not go out.

'Why are you cooped up here today?'

I lied to Padmini that there was no particular reason for that.

'He's unwell, he said. He's not coming.' Padmini stripped me of wellness without a trace of remorse, and flung her words across the fence.

I saw Sasankan walk away disappointed.

'So will it be done by tomorrow?' she asked while making the bed.

I hmmed.

'What's wrong?' She came up close and checked my forehead for fever.

'Ayyo, you are burning! You have fever!'

No, I shook my head.

'Just open your mouth, say something!' She was getting angry now.

'Nothing,' I said. 'It all ends tomorrow. Probably that's why …' I said that so she wouldn't holler any more.

'Oh, that is nothing. Just lie down and go to sleep,' she said, from her side of the cot.

When I had washed Kuttyamma that afternoon, her body that middle-age had not yet touched made my fingers erect. When I touched her nipples, the moonlight flowed from beneath my waist despite myself. As I rubbed each of her pores, the rocky layers of lust broke into crevices from which the water flowed. It was then that I heard someone panting behind me. Turning around, I saw the blind old pig. A thick sticky black liquid dripped from its tongue. I covered the nakedness of the statue quickly with a large piece of black cloth.

The pig moved away quickly, probably hearing the hunchbacked man's footsteps.

'So is it ready?' he asked.

I tried to smile.

'What are you thinking about? Please lie down, switch off the light!' Padmini had woken up from one cycle of sleep.

The light was switched off. When I was sure that she had fallen asleep again, I got up and went to the bathroom. Once again, beauty filled my fist.

11

I did not want to eat anything in the morning. A great fatigue had enveloped me.

'Eat something, won't you?' Padmini insisted.

I refused and got into the car. She stood at the doorstep rather unusually, watching me being driven away. She was happy that I was a proper fellow now, a hardworking artist. People here did not care when Sankara Pillai Saar tried to tell them: He may be just a carpenter, an Asari by birth, but after all he is an artist—won't he be frustrated? But Sasankan too said that some people were beginning to think that a sculptor was someone who was a bit extraordinary, someone who could preen around a little bit.

'This is my last day at work,' I told the car driver. He appeared not to have heard me. Every day I would drop a line or half, but he never replied. When he dropped me back, I thought, I must offer him a tip. He wouldn't accept it perhaps, but still.

That day, I thought, was somehow different. The pigs, the cock, the man who ran with the bull on his neck, the hunchbacked man—they were all missing, I noticed, as I walked towards my workshed. Even the gravelled yard, which normally murmured as I walked, seemed to have fallen silent. The forked tongues that leapt out to lick the car on other days now seemed to have been swallowed by the thickets. The silence made me feel like I was the only living soul there. I turned around—the man and the car were not there any more. The pounding of my heart filled my ears and the resonance nearly swallowed them. The black cat that normally sat atop the thatched roof of the workshed, too, was nowhere to be seen. As I neared it, an inexplicable fear wrapped itself tight around my legs. My feet began to drag. Then, the doors of my workshed split asunder, thrown open by a powerful blast of air; it thrust fear into my eyes. I saw the black cloth with which I had covered Kuttyamma take off like it had acquired a hundred thousand legs. The colour of darkness flew past the trees and plants and lost itself somewhere.

I stood petrified, rooted to the ground, my breath paralysed in wild awareness of the rising and falling tides of fear. Then mustering all my strength, I took one huge leap towards the workshed. A naked man, his body turned towards Kuttyamma's, his face pressed on her breasts, lying in her arms! In that moment, the Father and the Lover mated in me, and a certain madness was born into which I lurched and fell—and my hands found a heavy sledgehammer. With a force that was indeed unstoppable, I broke the man's head to pieces. And as I moved forward to break into bits the Great Phallus that had pulled up my adolescence and shoved it into unending envy, my arms froze in mid-air. Beneath that waist, inside the thicket of grey hair, a vagina—like the head of a serpent.

I looked at the face. The veil of blood had, by then, rendered it unseeable.

The Spectre

Unni and Ambili were walking back from school. Ambili felt the pee coming fast. She ran into the bushes, but came rushing back.

'You didn't pee?' Unni asked her.

'No. I saw this as I sat down,' said Ambili, showing him a small copper water-pot.

'What's this?'

'I don't know.'

Around the water-pot, the faint smell of verdigris lay like a small fence.

'Let's open it,' Ambili said.

Unni handed it back to her. 'You do it.'

'You're scared!'

Unni laughed.

Then they heard a sound from afar. Then another. And then yet another. As though some sounds were clambering up, hanging on to the legs of the first sound. When they came near, Unni and Ambili hid the pot.

'What are you two doing hiding there?' Kottayam Bhaskaran chettan stepped out of the group of people who were marching in a demonstration.

'Had to pee,' Unni said.

'Peed? So run home now.' Unni and Ambili took off. So did Bhaskaran chettan, to rejoin the demonstration.

'Radhe, at least try to find out where he is now.' Unni and Ambili reached their doorstep. That was the voice of Ammini Amma who ran the cornershop. She was giving their mother advice.

'Hey, you go inside. I'll hide this and be back soon. Tell Amma I went to pee if she asks.'

Ambili agreed, nodding her head.

Unni ran into the yam-patch and hid the pot there.

'Wonder if he's got tangled in some hook-up somewhere?' Ammini Amma sounded hesitant to ask. Amma looked like she was deaf.

Unni and Ambili put away their books and were sneaking out in the shade of Ammini Amma's chatter, when Amma called out, 'Where are you two off to?'

'To play,' said Ambili.

'Go change, wash your hands and legs first.'

'Can we do that after playing?' Unni asked.

'Listen to your mother, children,' Ammini Amma sounded piqued.

So they changed, washed, ate the steamed yam—and tore into the yard.

'Are you scared to open it?'

'You, you tried first—you try now too.'

Ambili loosened the cloth that bound the pot's mouth, and it now felt really heavy. It slipped from her hands and fell. They peered inside. There was something whitish around the pot's mouth. Suddenly it formed the outline of a tiny mouth. The tiny mouth began to make a big sound and let out a puff of smoke. Unni and Ambili stared as a shape began to take form from the smoke.

Unni grabbed Ambili's hand in fear, whispering, 'Oh, a Spectre!' and hid behind the jackfruit tree.

The form became distinct now. Long hair covering the ears. A long beard. A coat and trousers. Shoes.

'Ayye, what kind of Spectre is this?' Ambili was disappointed yet suspicious. Unni was suspicious too.

When the smoke had dispersed, the Spectre stood alone in the mouth of the pot, still as a statue. Unni picked up a pebble and threw it at the Spectre. He moved.

'Come,' Ambili called Unni, walking towards the Spectre.

'You go ahead,' he said.

They stood a little away from the Spectre.

'What's your name?' Ambili asked.

The Spectre did not respond.

'Didn't you hear? What's your name?' Unni was feeling bolder now.

'My name is Ambili. This fellow is Unni. Now tell us yours.'

The Spectre was still silent.

'Have you had any food?'

Silence.

Unni plucked a nutmeg and held it out.

'Don't eat the seed,' Ambili warned.

Just then Amma began to call, and her voice echoed all over the place, banging against the coconut and jackfruit trees.

'Get in, get in soon!' Ambili hurried it.

The Spectre looked at her uncomprehendingly. Unni pointed at the pot, and he went in. They tied up the mouth of the pot, hid it in the yam-patch, and ran to the house.

When they lay in bed, Unni worried about the scary creature that mothers made up to make their children obey: 'Will the wild-maakkaan get him?'

'Wild-maakkaans don't eat spectres. They're scared of them,' reassured Ambili.

They shut their eyes when Amma's sharp 'Sleep now!' crashed above their whispers. But because they knew that as usual, Amma would be sitting up all alone, wide awake in the dark, sleep did not come to their shut eyelids.

The next day was a Saturday—no school. Amma left for work before they woke up. She worked in the kitchen of the Brahmins—the Tekkedathu Mana people. Unni and Ambili got up, ran into the yard, and opened the pot. The Spectre rose up from inside the smoke.

'You're hungry?'

The Spectre did not say anything.

'I'll be back with some gruel,' Unni ran off.

'Where's your home?'

The Spectre kept looking at Ambili, but didn't say anything.

'Who shut you in this pot?'

He was still silent.

'Did your hair and beard grow long after you got locked inside?'

No words yet.

When Unni brought the gruel, the Spectre drank up all of it.

'Poor thing. Must have been really hungry.'

Ambili shook her head saying yes.

The gruel's starchy film hung on his moustache and beard like cobwebs. He brushed the cobwebs off. Some rice grains hid themselves in his beard.

'Did he tell you his name?'

'No.'

'Maybe he's deaf.'

'Ah, right!'

Ambili brought her slate and pencil and told the Spectre to write. He didn't understand, so she gestured. He wrote something, but they couldn't comprehend it.

'Poor thing can't write either!' Unni exclaimed.

'So what? We'll teach him! You go get your slate and pencil.'

A, Aaa—Ambili wrote the Malayalam alphabet. The Spectre copied it quickly. When he saw the Spectre learn the letters that quickly, Unni couldn't help wanting to be a spectre.

They made him write 'Ambili' and 'Unni.' Now write your name, Ambili wrote. The Spectre wrote his name. But they couldn't read it. So strange it was—a word they were seeing for the very first time.

The sound of footsteps from the frontyard of their house made them alert. 'Someone's coming,' Unni said.

'Maybe Amma,' Ambili whispered back.

They made the Spectre go back into the pot, and returned to the house.

Amma had laid out a mat on the veranda and was lying down.

'What happened, Amma?' asked Ambili.

'Nothing—please make me some chukku coffee for me.'
They went to the kitchen and made some.

Amma drank it and said, 'Now you can go and play.'
They didn't go. After some time, Amma fell asleep.
Ambili sat beside her, and Unni went to the yam-patch.
'Do you know where our father is?' he asked the Spectre.

The Spectre didn't reply.

'He went away sometime back. Hasn't returned yet.'

The Spectre looked into Unni's eyes. Unni didn't look back.

'I'll get you some gruel for supper,' he said.

Making the Spectre go back into the pot, Unni plucked a colocasia leaf to make a container for the evening's gruel, and then walked backed home.

They wanted to ask Amma what the Spectre had written on the slate. But, then, she would ask a hundred questions. So they didn't ask her.

All their friends in Class 4 tried reading it. None of them could manage. 'So hard to say,' some said. 'So hard to read,' said others.

Perhaps it's the name of a place, some thought. They decided to show the slate to the Malayalam master. He read the clumsy letters and asked, 'Who wrote this?'

Ambili stuttered and stammered, 'A ... a ... Spectre!' The master had a hearty laugh. He asked Ambili to come closer and told her to read it letter by letter. Then he told her to read it all together.

'It's ... ss ... ve'y ... har,' she stammered again.

'Be bold!' the master said. Ambili read it in a low whisper so that only he could hear.

'Clever girl!' he said. 'Now read aloud.'

Ambili looked at the teacher and then at everyone else, and read the letters on the slate together: 'Karl Marx.'

The name rang out and then hovered before the wonder-filled eyes of the children.

'We have a Petromax in our house,' someone piped up from the back of the class.

'This too is a light-giving Petromax,' said the master, laughing.

By the time they were on their way back from school, Unni and Ambili had forgotten the name.

'Oh, so hard to remember!' said Unni.

'I thought you'd remember.'

'You're the studious one. I forget everything very quickly.'

'Let's just call him Spectre,' she calmed him down.

Unni regaled his classmates with the stories Spectre told him and Ambili. They sang the songs he taught them in a strange tongue. When their friends asked what language they were singing in, 'Bhoothathinte bhasha,' 'Spectral Tongue,' Ambili told them, and generally felt quite proud.

Unni and Ambili played hide-and-seek with Spectre; also robber-and-police. And in-the-pond-on-the-bank. Every time, Spectre lost. Unni and Ambili won.

'Spectre is a sweetheart,' said Ambili.

'Yes, he doesn't even know how to hide when we play hide-and-seek,' Unni added.

When they bested him, a secret smile would form on Spectre's lips hidden under his whiskers and beard. A smile that no one could see.

One day, when Unni and Ambili came home from school, their grandmother was visiting. They called her Ammachyamma. She had bought bangles and a chain for Ambili and a plastic toy for Unni from the trinket shop. Unni peered through the double-eyepiece of the toy.

'Hey, edi, look, you can touch the shoe-flower plant near the well!'

Ambili looked through the eyepiece. The shoe-flower plant was just an arm's length away now!

They ran into the yard.

'You can see faraway things as if they are near,' said Unni and gave the toy to Spectre.

Spectre too peered through the toy's eyepiece.

In the distance, he saw a mourners' procession. Just a handful of people. Familiar faces. In the decorated coffin—*Eleanor*!

Spectre could not hold back his tears. It was the first time Unni and Ambili were seeing a grown-up cry. They couldn't comprehend why he was crying.

Looking out from the yard, they could see the hovels of folk poorer than them—really poor people. Maybe he wept seeing them, they decided and returned home. Ammachyamma and Amma were sitting on the veranda.

'What did the bank people say?' Ammachyamma asked.

'No more extension,' Amma said.

'I have spoken with Chandran. He will take Unni. You should not object any more. He is, after all, his uncle.'

Amma's silence made the darkness in the house darker still. Ammachyamma kept talking. Unni and Ambili fell asleep without hearing the rest.

Amma went to school when they were having the mid-day meal of rice-gruel. Unni saw her first. They finished quickly and got up.

'So have you finally decided to shift the children?' the headmaster asked.

'What choice do I have, sir?'

'Both are such good learners,' said the headmaster. 'This fellow is a little lazy, though.'

Unni shrank behind Amma.

'Won't it be sad to separate them?' The headmaster's voice faltered a bit.

Amma nodded.

On the way back home, she said to the children, 'You shouldn't be upset.'

They did not reply.

'I'll be very sad if you cry.'

'We won't,' said Ambili, holding Amma's hand tight.

'So we don't have a house of our own any more?' Unni asked.

'There are many in this world who don't have a house of their own,' Amma said with equanimity.

They had heard her say this at other times, so they nodded.

Their little legs hurried to catch up with her.

'I am going with Amma to Ammachyamma's house. He's going to Amma's older brother's house,' Ambili told Spectre.

'There are many in this world who don't have a house of their own,' Unni said.

Hearing this, Spectre closed his eyes for a moment.

'There are many in this world who have no food,' said Ambili.

Unni was amazed hearing her say that.

'Who told you this?'

'Amma, when I left food on the plate the other day.'

'Ah, right,' Unni recalled.

They slipped out without Amma noticing, took the pot and ran towards the Raviswaram paddy field. Standing on the raised strip of land that ran through its middle, they opened the pot's mouth. Spectre came out. The three of them stood there wordlessly. Seeing the tears in Spectre's eyes, Ambili struggled to control her own and said, 'Amma doesn't like to see anyone cry. Neither do we.'

Spectre tried to smile at the strength that brimmed in those words. For the first time, Unni and Ambili saw him smile.

'We have to get back before Amma calls,' Unni said.

Spectre put his arms around them. They all smiled.

Unni and Ambili ran home. Spectre rose higher and higher into the sky. The crows, seeing a strange and massive bird, panicked. They tried futilely to peck and strike at Spectre. The crowd that gathered below seeing the melee above screamed in pure terror, thinking that a spectre was out to get them. Only the little children laughed, seeing a huge big butterfly in the sky. They held up their arms and waved to him, saying, 'Come, come—come down to the earth.'

Satanic Verses

Kunhikkannu had two roosters, Vladimir and Bukharin. Bukharin has been missing for some days. He's searched for him everywhere—in the Raviswaram fields, the Vattakkottai Fort, in the two abandoned wells. He even brought a light to check on the Ilavu tree in the churchyard and the tamarind tree behind the toddy shop at night. Bukharin was not found.

Vladimir and Bukharin wouldn't venture past the small space around the house. When Kunhikkaanu stepped out, they would go with him till the gate, jabbering furiously. Kunhikkannu would turn to those who heard them with the smile that came to him so naturally and say, 'You won't understand, this is Russian!'

Like Kunhikkannu, Vladimir too fell into deep sadness. He stopped gadding about in the yard. He would look at the grains of rice, but not peck at them. He rested all the time on the half-wall of the veranda or the bundles of paper inside. Those who saw the exhaustion in Kunhikkannu's eyes and gait tried to tell him affectionately—Kunhikkanne, how can you go on like this, without even sipping some water! Please eat something. He responded to all of them by putting on a beaming smile.

It was the ploughman Owtha who asked how a cock could have crossed the yard and the fields, and got past the canal beyond. What if he had gone out of the house and lost his way? What if he was hiding somewhere in fear, his beak shut, Kunhikkannu shot his counter-questions. That's possible too, admitted Owtha.

People remembered the disappearance of Kunhikkannu's rooster in the middle of things—sitting in their houses, the churchyard, the toddy shop, and the ration shop—and then Bukharin, who was a strapping fellow with a luxuriant long tail and a fine comb on his head, would spring up in everybody's memory, crowing loudly.

When the newly-weds in the village or guests or small children were puzzled by the sight of a thin, tall old man walking all over the yards and fields there, peering at the branches of trees and calling out, 'Hey Bukharin, hey Bukharin,' the locals would tell them his story. 'That man? His name is Kunhikkannu. His house is by the canal. He's looking for his rooster. Was a friendly chap, always smiling and chatting with everyone—just look at him now. He barely talks. Not married. Pretty advanced in years. Ask him and he'll say, two hundred years old! Don't be misled by his thinness. He's as strong as a tree-trunk. Used to be a master at arm-wrestling. He's been on ships and has walked in the desert! The two roosters are named after two chaps who were with him in those days. Can't read or write, but makes a living selling books! Stores plenty of books and magazines in his house. Ask him why, and he gives this funny reply—that some books are unique, just like the earth and the sky. Ask him how he knows, and he'll just roll his head, wink, and smile—that's just how it is.

Nobody could see why Kunhikkannu would have complained to the police about a cock gone missing. Since the past half-hour, they had been waiting in front of his house. Someone told them, very reluctantly, that Kunhikkannu was seen standing under the jackfruit tree near the shop. Some others ran to find him. In the end, they found him in the rubber plantation, sitting on the ground, eyes closed. As he accompanied them, Kunhikkannu's eyes were climbing up and down the yards and trees all the way back to his house. They all wanted to tell him: Kunhikkannu, walk faster, the police are waiting. But no one uttered a word. There were people in the group who were doubtful whether the police would be able to find the missing rooster. They too stayed quiet. As for Kunhikkannu, he said nothing.

Vladimir saw the police take Kunhikkannu away from the half-wall of the veranda. He did not understand why his master was being taken away. The locals got to know later that he had been picked up not for losing the cock, but for encroaching on the road while selling his books. When one of them asked why someone who had been selling his books there for the past forty years or so had suddenly been picked up now, everyone agreed that it was suspicious.

Kunhikkannu was made to stand in the middle of a circle of really senior police officers. His answers to their questions were all utterly truthful. His parents had died early. He then moved around all over India, did many odd jobs, finally ending up in a plantation in Munnar. On hearing that A.K. Gopalan was on a hunger strike in Amaravathi, he left the job and went there. After the struggle, he went to Thalassery and joined the circus as a clown. Later he started selling books. He didn't go to the mosque. Nor did he pray otherwise. Had ten cents of land, a house and two roosters. One of them had gone missing a few days back.

But the police did not want to know any of this. How was the illiterate Kunhikkannu in the business of selling books? Kunhikkannu turned to a policeman and asked him innocently for his name and address. The policeman told him his address. He turned to another policeman, and he too responded. Then Kunhikkannu told the first policeman, 'Saar, your name is Ramesan and your home is in Kudamalloor. This saar is Muhammad, from Thazhathangadi. Books too are like human beings. You just need to like them to meet them.' One of the police officers, who found this amusing, let out a low laugh.

'Where did you get this from?' A policeman showed him a book.

Kunhikkannu looked at it from behind the webs of his cataracts.

'It was in your shop; we found it when we broke into it,' said the policeman who had laughed earlier.

'This was not in the shop, saar,' said Kunhikkannu.

The policeman now laughed loudly, then called him closer and asked menacingly, 'So then how did it get there, you tell us? It doesn't have arms or legs to go there on its own!'

Kunhikkannu looked at him but said nothing.

'Tell us!' the policeman roared.

'Saar, that's what I used to believe as well. But these days, I think books have arms and legs and ears and more. They can open their mouths, and breathe too. Do you know, saar, some of them disappear all of a sudden, some hide from us! They hide so well, you'd think them gone. Then they come back, and someone finds them again!'

The senior policeman looked amused again. He drank a glass of water and fixed his eyes on Kunhikkannu's face for some time.

'Where did you get this book? Who did you buy it for? How many copies of it have you sold till now? How many are left with you? Did you know that this is a prohibited book?' These questions hurtled towards poor

Kunhikkannu. Unable to answer, he felt weak. Even in that exhaustion, he looked at the table, amazed that there was a book lying on it that could not be sold or read. The book was now looking at him. He smiled. It smiled back. The policemen didn't see that.

Everyone got to know that Kunhikkannu was remanded. Everyone except Vladimir. He passed his days waiting for Kunhikkannu and Bukharin to return, perching alternately on the veranda's half-wall and the roof.

In the cell, Kunhikkannu's companions were the thief Sankaran and the bootlegger Gabriel. Sankaran was dumb and mostly deaf too. Gabriel and he communicated not through sign language but by writing in the air. Why was he erasing letters written in the air—that was Kunhikkannu's only doubt. 'Why, won't someone else read them if you left them there,' replied Gabriel. 'How could that be, I can't see anything,' Kunhikkannu said. And then Gabriel asked him to write his name in the air. Kunhikkannu told him that he couldn't read or write. Gabriel smiled back saying, 'I will teach you.'

Gabriel took Kunhikkannu's finger and made him write the letters in the air. In between, when the memory of Vladimir and Bukharin came to him, or when age took away his memory, his writing would go wrong. Gabriel would then punish him, making him write those letters a hundred or two hundred times over. Kunhikkannu would obey.

One morning Gabriel woke him up from sleep, wrote something in the air, and asked him to read it. Straining through the cobwebs of his cataract, Kunhikkannu looked at the writing and pronounced his name in a voice lowered by age. That made Gabriel very happy. Sankaran the thief was sound asleep and so did not know a thing.

When he had nothing else to do, Kunhikkannu would write in the air—'Vladimir', 'Bukharin'. In the Malayalam letters, the 'l' hid under the 'v' like a kitten when he tried to write 'vla'. He asked Sankaran and Gabriel many times about it. They both didn't know all that much and so didn't say anything. Kunhikkannu, however, liked that kittenish curl a lot. So he would write now and then—'vla'. The kitten beneath the 'v' would purr softly every time, only for him.

When they stood in the veranda of the court, Kunhikkannu made out every single word Gabriel wrote in the air. Will we get bail? Don't know, he wrote back. They stood there for longer than usual. Hearing the policemen talk agitatedly to each other and seeing a scared expression spread on their faces, he asked Gabriel: What's up? Gabriel shut out the crowd's hum and focused on the policemen's talk.

Gabriel wrote: They have lost the stolen goods. What? Kunhikkannu asked. Your book, Gabriel wrote back. Kunhikkannu nodded, winked, and smiled. Gabriel couldn't make out what that smile meant. Kunhikkannu whispered: Someone killed Bukharin. But there are some things that can't be wiped out. That too went over Gabriel's head. Write, said he. Kunhikkannu wrote. Gabriel read it. Full of mistakes, he scolded. You have to have 'd' not 't' in 'killed'. And it is 'wiped' not 'wibed'.

Kunhikkannu lifted up his finger and began to write in the air the phrases with the correct spellings, over and over again.

He Who Went Alone

Like most of Unni's stories, this too is set in a village in the south-eastern district of Kottayam in Kerala, which has a rich history of spiritual revival of the Dalit Pulaya community since the 19th century. Conversion of the Pulayas into Christianity by the missionaries of the Church Missionary Society brought little respite to the terrible caste oppression they suffered, and in the early 20th century, a gifted Pulaya spiritual leader, Poikayil Yohannan (later known as Appachan—'Father'—to his followers) broke away from Protestant Christianity to shape a new liberating spiritual-material order called the Pratyaksha Raksha Daiva Sabha, braving enormous opposition and violence by the upper caste elite. The new visionaries did their work at great risk, hiding in the wildernesses and staying constantly on the move. This area is also resonant with Pulaya myths of power, like the story of the Paraya chief of Pallam and the legendary warrior, Chengannuraady. 'He Who Went Alone' draws on this fascinating web of history and myth.

They had wandered wearily, knocked on the doors of many, tried many different excuses. Everywhere people had thrown up their hands and said to them: No way! This is the first day of the month. So sorrowful the whole business was that Chandran and Govindan were quite inconsolable. Now they sat, legs dangling, staring into the darkness approaching from the other side of dusk. Let our throats not stay parched, they entreated. At the end of the prayer, Govindan said, 'There's a way.' Chandran looked anxiously at him, almost fearing that the 'way' might dissipate on its way out of Govindan's mouth.

'There's a bottle of stuff in Father's cupboard. Saw when I wen' there to repair th' door y'day.'

Chandran looked scared. 'Steal from th' parish house?'

When Govindan explained that just as it was not wrong for the thirsty to take water or for the hungry to take food, so too it was not wrong for two drinkers to take a bottle of liquor that no one seemed to want, and that this would actually be the liberation of liquor unto its true duty, Chandran could only gape.

Govindan also warned Chandran not to step too hard on the sixth plank of the wooden staircase of the parish house because it was loose. They climbed the steps without loosening the plank, opened the window and slipped inside through it, tiptoed without waking Father, opened the almirah which let out a low growl as the key turned, took the bottle, and slipped back out. On the way,

Chandran also picked up the water-jug and glass that were lying on the veranda.

Shrugging off the wild vines and the *communist-paccha* weeds that hugged their legs, they went off to the eastern corner of the graveyard, and sat down on one of the gravestones. When the liquor flowed, Chandran looked towards the south and started counting: 'Karikkaaran Mathai, ove' there; Ely chechi, next to him; to her side, Philippose chettan ... Then ... wha' about this stone we're sittin' on?'

Govindan lifted his bums a bit, wiped the dust off the grave, struck a match, and looked. He saw the dates of birth and death of one Thundiyil Mathai.

'Under us,' said Govindan, lowering the flame closer to the gravestone, 'is a fellow who died a ba' death—Mathaichan, of Thundiyil.

'*Entammo*! Tha' was sixteen slashes—couldn't bear to look at the head an' face, such a state he wa' in!' Chandran remembered aloud. 'All sixteen from that billhook!'

Govindan took the glass from Chandran and asked, 'It's been two years since Akkiri jumped parole—how come they haven't got 'im all this time?'

Chandran lowered his voice. 'He's a low-caste Pulaya ... he must 'ave done some *odi*-magic ... some witchery ... Or else how did Mathaichan, who was sleeping at home, walk all the way up to the churchyard and get sliced thin with the billhook?'

After downing the last gulp and throwing away the bottle, they decided to be decent and return the jug and glass. And so they crossed the churchyard and were about to step on the path to the parish house when, out of the church came a man with a long beard and flowing hair. Chandran started, and dropped the jug. The man walked soundlessly on the gravelled yard of the church. Govindan followed him. Chandran was terrified, but he too went along. Try as they might, he was impossible to catch up with. So aiming to waylay him at the junction, they jumped the low wall of the south-side yard, ran down the Puliveli family's fields and reached just across the canal. The frail and tall form was walking westward through the mud-path in the field. Govindan drew in a frightened breath and exclaimed, 'Ayyo, isn't that our Yesu?'

Chandran collapsed to the ground that very moment.

When it was nearly dawn, the two of them walked home silently, along the bank of the canal. Then they saw people on the Akkara-chira, the raised land on the other side of the canal, with their cows and goats and fowls. 'Where are you going so early?' Govindan and Chandran called out to them.

'We aren't going—just bringing back all that went missing,' Balan Pillai hollered back, holding a duck in each hand. 'When we woke up this morning, they were gone. We went searching and found them crowded on the steps of our ferry-landing!'

'My dear Govinda,' shouted Janaki Amma who was leading back her cows, 'You should've seen how these cows were standin' there ... still and starin' across the water ... as if they were seein' off som'one!'

Govindan heard that and turned to look at Chandran.

Amidst stories circulating about how the tamarind tree of the Pidika family had split exactly into two last night, how the hundred-year-old rain-shade of the Palakaashery people lay in the dust this morning, and how the banana tree, heavy with fruit, had turned overnight into a burnt, blackened cinder, Govindan and Chandran quietly went to the house of Raman Kaniar. Kaniar took out his *kavadi*-set and laid it out to divine the mystery. 'There's something amiss in the air here,' he declared. In the end, the two told him flatly, 'Kaniare, looks like Yesu's left our church ... need to do a *prasnam* to find out ...'

'Ayyo, Govinda!' said Kaniar. 'I can manage if our Devi or Sivan, or Ganapathy run away ... but this is an English god, no?'

By noon, when Chandran and Govindan slunk back home without telling anyone what they'd seen, fearing everybody's ire, the frail and tall form had gone past the Idukki Bus-Stand, past the Idukki Dam, past the statue of Kolumban Muthan, the Grand Old Man of the tribes who showed builders the way to the site, and walked along the bank of the river and into the deep forest. When it reached the little hut built close to the river, it stopped.

Hearing a pair of feet shuffling outside his hut, Akkiri hid the billhook behind his back and peeped through the screwpine-matting. The sight outside was yet to reach Akkiri, when the sound came close to him: 'It's me, Yesu.'

Akkiri dropped his billhook and went out. 'Why've you come this way?'

'The believers are always fightin' over there.'

'Oh-yuh-won'-let-oth'rs-get-sumpeace-even-here,' murmured Akkiri, glaring at Yesu. The sweaty exhaustion of his journey could be seen on Yesu.

'Did yuh eat sumthin'?'

No, Yesu shook his head.

'So go an' 'ave a bath. I'll fix sumthin.' '

Handing him a towel and a badly faded lungi, Akkiri pointed to a stone some distance away outside the hut and said, 'There's a scrub-bark there, in case you wan'to rub yerself clean.'

Yesu went to the river. Akkiri went off to chop firewood. The wood split like butter when the sharpness of the axe lowered its face lightly into it. He finished the job and returned, but Yesu was nowhere to be seen. Where's he gone now, thought Akkiri, and went looking. Yesu was standing by the river, looking at the water.

'Yuh didn't 'ave yer bath?'

'I can't swim,' said Yesu.

'So?'

'Can only walk on water.'

Akkiri went and fetched a pot. 'Fill it with water and pour it on your head.'

When they were drinking gruel, Akkiri didn't look at Yesu. Yesu yearned for his glance while they supped. But strangely, today, Akkiri's attention was focussed on every grain of cooked rice before him.

'Won't the police ... come ... lookin'?' Yesu asked, haltingly.

Akkiri continued to drink his gruel. A few moments passed, and Yesu asked again, 'Six more years ... right?'

Akkiri downed the rest of the gruel in one gulp, wiped his lips, and looked at Yesu.

'Will y' be at peace if I go bac'to jail for the rest o' the six years?'

'No' that ...' Before Yesu could finish what he was saying, Akkiri kicked aside the salt-pot.

'Remembe' what Mathaichan had said when we were buryin' my father?'

Yesu said nothing.

'That a Pulaya couldn't be buried wher' their fathers were sleepin'.'

Yesu still said nothing.

'My appan was buried in a hole in the mud, in soggy land. They say eve'now, I killed him for that? Yuh kno'well wha'appened—the churches quarrelled, and those fellows from Kaipuzha killed 'im right befor' yer eyes? Yuh jus' looked on tha'day? Why didn't yuh save me? Because we're converts—new Christians?'

Yesu looked away.

When he picked up his bowl and began to walk away, Akkiri asked, 'Why shoul I be in jail?'

Yesu drew a cross with the leaf-spoon in his gruel, not meaning anything in particular.

When dusk fell, Akkiri picked up the fishing rod and went to the river. Before he left, he told Yesu to chop and cook the tapioca, and crush some kanthari chillies.

He was amazed. Today the fish jumped to bite his bait smiling. Usually, they came only after a whole hour, gobbling up all the bait. Wonder who they're all coming to meet today, he thought as he returned home with them on his stake. He was met by the scent of cooked tapioca and crushed chillies. Akkiri smiled at Yesu for the first time ever. He then looked around. There was no sign of tapioca peel; the grinding-stone showed no sign of having been used; not even a fire had been lit.

'So yuh just said, "Tapioca, get cooked", an' "Chillies, get crushed", right?'

'Um-hum,' agreed Yesu.

'A'right, do this. Get the tapioca an' the knife and come out here.'

Yesu got both and followed Akkiri.

After they had had supper, Akkiri sat outside on a low branch and smoked. He came in to lie down when he had finished. He lowered the flame of the hurricane lamp and peeped out of the screwpine-matting of the hut. Yesu was standing outside, his gaze fixed on the far distance. Akkiri went out to see what he was staring at.

> *Appan's nowher',* thin-thaa-ra
> *Orphans ar' we,* thin-thaa-ra
> *Where're we goin',* thin-thaa-ra
> *Appan's bee' sold,* thin-thaa-ra
> *Amma's bee' sold,* thin-thaa-ra …

Someone was singing tunefully. Others too sang after him. 'Do you know the man who's singing?' Yesu asked Akkiri. No, Akkiri shook his head. 'That is Appachan,' said Yesu. Yes, indeed, Poikayil Appachan, He who freed the Pulaya spirit from slavery nearly a hundred years ago. He who gathered those who were condemned to be wretched into the bosom of faith. They are coming from the past. On the left is Barnabas, Vaazhel Ouseph; on the right, Vellangur Daniel, Koottikkal Kurien, Aaryaaliyil Mathai and Valyapuraikkal Chacko—his disciples. They are returning from the Great Coming-Together of the Pulaya faithfuls at Kulathur, triumphant, braving the strong arm of the proud and the decadent. Akkiri stood there, watching Appachan and his companions walk along singing and disappear in the distance. Much after they had left, their song lingered—until Akkiri fell asleep.

He woke up late the next day and lay on the mat, unable to recall who he had seen last night.

Yesu brought him coffee. 'No' miracle coffee,' he said.

Akkiri took it from him smiling. 'Wha' did we see last night?'

'Wha' all?'

'Hey, didn't yuh show me Appachan?'

'Will tell yuh if yuh teach me how to swim!'

Akkiri taught Yesu how to swim. Yesu showed him Appachan's childhood. Akkiri taught Yesu how to cook fish. Yesu told him about Chengannuraadi, the bravest of the Pulayas in all of history. Akkiri taught Yesu to climb trees. Yesu showed him the Great Parayan of Pallam. Akkiri taught Yesu how to fish. Yesu showed him Appachan singing at Changanashery:

> *No word of God*
> *is heard*
> *No Divine Messenger*
> *in sight*
> *No God's worker*
> *to show the way*
> *Oh, I saw no God*
> *I saw no Yesu*
> *The soul, the angels,*
> *I did not see,*
> *My eyes,*
> *they did not see.*

When they were about to go to bed that night, Yesu asked, 'How long can you stay here this way?'

'Oh leave that,' shrugged Akkiri, 'D'yuh know what day it's tomorrow?'

Yesu shook his head to say no.

'Good Friday.'

'Oh my God,' Yesu laughed out loud. 'I actually forgot, yuh know?'

'Sha' we celebrate?'

'Why not!' said Yesu.

When Akkiri woke up the next morning, his fingers were tightly locked with Yesu's. Akkiri extricated them, taking care not to wake him.

'I'll get some country booze an' pork,' said Akkiri, after their morning coffee. 'Cook the tapioca before I return.'

'I don't drink country-brew,' said Yesu.

'Okay, today yuh work a miracle. Turn the water boilin' there into wine,' Akkiri said and chuckled.

When he left, Yesu swept their hut clean, washed their clothes, caught fish, and cooked the tapioca.

'Who's moved in with you?' asked Ousep, who grew cannabis on the Randaam Hill, pouring out Akkiri the liquor.

'From bac' home.'

'Not a Judas, mole-guy?'

'No, jus' a sole-guy.'

Ousep hmmed.

When he came down the hill and reached the slope sweeping down below, Akkiri saw some shadows which, in a moment, disappeared into the distance. He caught his breath, hid behind the bushes, and then began to climb down very carefully. When he reached behind a large tree at some distance from the hut, the shadows grew solid.

'So what did you think? That we wouldn't catch you if you hid in the forest growing a beard and your hair?'

Yesu was silent.

The sub-inspector pulled out his belt and whipped him hard on the back. The policeman in front shoved his lathi hard below his navel. At this, Akkiri almost jumped out of the shade behind the tree, but Yesu shook his head and signalled: No.

The belt flew through the air once more and fell on Yesu's throat. And along with it, came a loud snarl—'Walk!'

Yesu took one step forward. Akkiri looked at him and Yesu returned his gaze. Watching Yesu and the policemen climb the hill and disappear, Akkiri's exhausted body sagged against the tree.

On the third day, before dawn, he went back home, swimming across the Meenachil River. The wind began to wail in the trees.

Hearing the cow moo unendingly in its shed, Govindan ran out. His wife and children who followed him, saw him stand at the edge of the yard, staring. 'What happened?' they asked.

Pointing to the path on which the branch of a jackfruit tree nearly touched the ground, Govindan said, 'There … tha' way … something's shinin' … movin' … there …'

His wife and children were simply blank.

That Thing

'Let it get darker,' I said.

My wife fixed me with a glare. I looked away, pretending not to see.

'Awful creature! Howling again!'

I pretended not to hear.

'It'll break out of the carton any moment now,' she murmured angrily.

I kept quiet.

I could hear its cries. I could see it writhe and struggle inside the box.

My wife was hurrying time up. And time was running fast.

'It's past ten.'

The hands of the clock had not yet reached ten; she was lying.

I got up from the chair and picked up the box.

'This time, make sure you throw it somewhere far away,' she said. 'Make sure it doesn't come back like the last time.'

I nodded.

Wondering what I would do if it broke out of the box and escaped, I paused a moment.

'Can you stop dawdling and do this quickly?'

I did not turn around. The door shut behind me harshly.

Should I turn left or right, I hesitated. The last time, I took the road to the right and left it in the garbage dump behind the market. There would be no dearth of food, I had thought. And it was cute, and so someone might spot it and take it home. Or else it would find some free-roaming fellows for friends. But within two days, we heard it purr near the kitchen. It was near the door, looking up pitifully. I felt sad. Not showing my sadness, I asked it quite sternly, 'How did you manage to find your way back?'

It smiled even in the middle of its misery, as if telling me that finding the way back was a cinch.

I fed it rice and fish. It licked the plate clean. Not once did it even lift its head.

It had become thinner in just two days.

We were together when my wife returned. 'So the damned thing's back!' she said, and kicked it hard. I escaped the kick only because of my innate human reflex.

It lay outside, mewing towards heaven.

'You're inviting God's wrath,' I said.

'I'm ready for that,' she fumed.

I did not go out to check on it. It got up, went over to the coconut tree, and lay down under it. I looked through the window. The poor thing lay there with its eyes shut.

'I'll kill it if it comes inside the house again!'

I only nodded.

'Don't come inside,' I told it. 'Don't know whom she meant—you or me—but she will kill, she said.'

It stayed in the shed outside.

Today, when my wife was away and I was reading the papers, I heard a grating sound, like someone were scratching the door. I put down the papers and looked. There it was, standing behind the door. 'Come in,' I said. It entered and came up to me very reluctantly. It rubbed its body on my legs. I read the papers aloud. It purred and mewed gently, snuggled up between my feet, and soon dozed off. I too dozed off after a while.

I woke up hearing a loud howl. My wife stood there, pointing to a box in the corner of the room, snarling: 'Make sure you throw it somewhere tonight itself!'

I took the left turn and walked on. The path was more or less empty. A star seemed to be watching from high above now and then. Or maybe that was my imagination. I had no torch with me. There were a few lights on the road, but even they were like asthma patients, wheezing heavily as they drew in and let out light.

Forgive me, I begged silently. It mewed. It was trying to tell me that it was alright, and I took solace in that. I wanted to ask if it would come back home again, but I held back. It, too, probably wanted to ask if I was really abandoning it. Neither of us spoke.

After a while, I realised that I was on a road that was totally dark. That scared me. It mewed again. It was telling me not to be scared, I comforted myself.

'Where are you headed in the middle of the night?' That was a female voice.

I froze in my tracks.

'Don't be scared.'

I noticed then that it wasn't really a woman's voice.

'Don't harm me,' I said, truly frightened now. That elicited a tinkling laughter.

'Harm you? Am I a policeman to harm you?'

I felt a bit relieved, but unsure what to do next, I stood still in the dark.

'Let's walk,' he said. I nodded, but he didn't catch that in the dark.

As our eyes began to adjust to the darkness, we looked at each other's faces. A young man, clean-shaven, with a hint of coyness on his lips. I tried to smile. He lowered his head, suddenly overcome by diffidence.

'What's this you're holding?' he asked.

'A cat.'

Without looking up, he asked, 'Where are you taking it?'

'I want to throw it away.'

He raised his head now. Scared to look into his eyes, I now lowered mine. There was no reason for me to lower my head, but that's what I did.

'Where will you throw it?'

'I don't know.'

Inside the box, it cried.

'Poor cat,' he said.

'Yes,' I said, 'poor thing.'

We were silent for a few moments. Noticing the lights of a vehicle from afar, he quickly pulled me into the shade of a tree.

'Police,' he whispered in my ear.

'So what?' I asked.

He did not answer. But right then, I felt his breath on my face.

The cat mewed from inside the box in my hands.

'Will the police hear us?' I asked.

'Maybe ...' Before he completed that sentence, he clapped my mouth shut with his palms. They smelled of scented talcum. The fingers pressed on my mouth were soft and warm, like a kitten's body.

When the jeep had passed us, he removed his hands. We looked at each other and smiled.

He took the box from me and opened it. It came out, looking wearied. It saw my face. And the star high up above. And his face, too, as though it were a familiar one. It mewed affectionately, and he petted it.

'My wife hates cats,' I said, sounding guilty.

'What about you?' he asked, his gaze entering deep into my eyes. Laughter was slowly filling his eyes. They glistened with mischief, like a kitten's eyes.

'What's its name?' he asked.

'It has no name,' I said.

'May I take it?' He held it close.

I said yes with my eyes.

'What's your name?' he asked.

'Chandran.'

He gave it a kiss and turned to me. 'Shall I call him Chandran?'

A firefly flitted into the space between us and flew away.

Caw

I always wanted to be a hunter. And so I kept with me for a very long time, the picture of a man in a round hat, with a rifle in his hand, his leg pressing down triumphantly on a tiger he had shot. Though I had no round hat or rifle, I too became a hunter by sheer desire. I aimed stones at big black ants, whacked cockroaches, snared squirrels. I killed. Some hens that came foraging in my yard were killed by my hand with a single stone. Dogs and cats did not come anywhere close to my house. They probably feared my aim.

But I lacked the gravitas of a hunter. That was one of my greatest regrets. It is true that the image of the hunter concealed behind leafy thickets, feet moving noiselessly, breath drawn in soundlessly, with all his five senses focussed on a single prey, still fascinated me. Whenever I felt weak, the animal scent of the memory of the hunter roused me to action.

I have envied the unshaken muscular face of Ahab, resolute in the face of the raging typhoon, from *Moby Dick*.

The look on his face as he stood with his foot pressed on the deck of his vessel—it must have been that look which, with feet pressed on the dead prey, sought to immobilize heaven and earth with fear in a single glance. As I relived the scene in my mind, I was able to experience the single-minded journey, the cruel meditation, that all hunters in the world, at all times, experience. All hunters begin that journey moments before they bring down their prey. A thrill would climb up from my little toe and spread all over my body. Once, I brought down a kitten near our kitchen with a stone. I had stood, pressed against the kitchen wall, stone in hand. It was then that I realised how important it was to be accurate. How the movements of my body, my breath, my vision, the strength of my fingers, all of it had to be concentrated entirely on the stone. I had just a few moments to decide where to hit—on the legs, forehead, or eye. I struck when it lowered its head to eat a fish-head. Before it could even lick the fish-head, it collapsed and rolled over, tongue still sticking out greedily. I pressed my foot on its small body and drew myself up. Small hunters can afford only such tiny pleasures. But at that very moment, a crow dropped its shit on my head. The shit fell on my nose, then my lips, and on my shirt. My face, on which revulsion had etched an ugly grimace, soon began to lose its seriousness and looked as if it was about to burst into tears. I looked up. There was a crow laughing at me. Not laughing. Deriding.

The body of the kitten under my feet moved for a second then. It raised its head to draw one last breath, threw me a glance, an I-don't-care look of utter contempt, really, and died. I was furious. I kicked it over and over again. And then, I shouted at the crow: 'Get lost, you mangy dog!'

I have hated crows since my childhood. I knew it for the first time as the wily creature that stole sweetmeats from children. I hated its crooked looks, its blackness, its horrible cawing. I tried many times to take aim at crows with stones, but they always managed to dodge my missiles in a flash. It was the speed with which they could move their bodies, which exceeded the speed of human thoughts, that always defeated me. Besides that, a crow had laughed mockingly at me once ... So crows became my sworn enemies for life.

Once, at school, a teacher had asked each of us to name our favourite birds. 'Parrot,' 'Mynah,' 'Cuckoo,' said many. Just one voice, from the backmost bench said, 'Crow.' The other students tittered over that voice and flew off like birds. The dark-skinned Dasan thus came to be known as Crow-Dasan. Gradually, I began to see a crow in him. His sneaky look, hair like a crow's feathers, nose as sharp as a crow-beak, and that voice, *kraa kraa*. One day when we were let out of the class to pee, I took aim at him. The stone hit his forehead, and he stumbled to the ground bleeding. In a flash—don't know where they came from—an army of crows descended, cawing loudly. Some of them took positions on the branches of trees close by. Some formed a cordon around him. I hid behind the door of the urinal and peeped out. It was truly scary. A friend of mine later said, 'Crow-Dasan's father is an *odi*-sorcerer.'

I quit that school. That wasn't the only reason, though it was a big enough reason. I began to feel that a crow was trailing me. In the bathroom, bedroom, on the bus—I felt that there was a crow watching me, only me. That's when I got myself a double-barrelled gun. The crow that teased me constantly, I was able to shoot down before it could flit aside and fly away. I remembered the fierceness with which once crows had, some years back, cordoned off a crow-chick that had fallen off the tamarind tree near our house. I knew well their menacing alertness, and so I buried the insolent crow that I had shot as fast as I could. Not even a single crow knew it was dead. 'They can't find out because it is the Emergency,' I had joked with my wife.

Now I live in a new housing colony that was built on paddy fields, ponds, canals, and marshes—all filled, smothered, and converted. My decision to live here was influenced by the way the builder had advertised it. The ad had an image of a foetus in the womb. It promised security and cleanliness.

After a couple of months, a few residents began to have problems with their electric connections. Some residents found pieces of meat and bones at their doorsteps. Yet others heard sharp knocks on their windows at night. For those who had chosen the housing colony purely for the security it had offered, this was unnerving. The police arrived and decided that all this was being done by those who had been evicted for the project, or by the people who used to fish in these areas for a living before.

In my own inquiry, I found that those people were so meek they couldn't even break a light-bulb; and besides, they were scattered and disunited. My suspicion, from Day 1, fell on the crows. Because I knew of their wiles, and their ability to nurse a grudge. I believed that strongly, and also told the other residents about it. In the beginning, a few paid attention; some even scoffed.

One night, the wife of the Colony Residents' Association President came running to my house. The sound of a crow cawing in her bedroom, apparently! It was then that I picked up my gun again, after many years. When I went there, no sound could be heard, except for the alarm of a clock that sounded like a cock crowing. I comforted her saying that it was probably just a feeling. But deep inside, I knew that a crow was hiding somewhere.

The next morning, the roads in the colony were all soaked with crow-shit. This sight triggered an emergency meeting of the Residents' Association. 'Destroy all the crows,' I suggested. 'Do away with the whole race.' The others stared in shock. 'There are many animal races that do not exist any more on the face of the earth,' I told them, 'like Steller's Sea Cow and the Spectacled Coromorant.'

Finishing off a single species wasn't a big deal, I proved to them with these examples. They were all sceptical about the means of wiping out the crows altogether. But their disgust towards crows, their colour and their jagged, sharp cawing, brought ugly scowls on their faces. They prayed that such mass extinction may be possible.

We sought out trees where crows had made nests and chopped them down. We broke all their eggs. For the first time, we allowed a heap of waste to accumulate in our exceptionally clean colony. The crows that descended there dropped dead eating poisoned left-overs. Those that tried to escape were shot down. We cast large nets which fell on them, trapping whole flocks. Within a month, we became a completely crow-less colony.

I had an extraordinary experience when I aimed at the last crow. We had thought that all crows were finally dead; but then, one landed on the road, ran through the colony, and started pecking the ground and loitering about quite nonchalantly. I quickly reached the spot on being informed, and took aim. Quite unexpectedly, it swung around, flew up and perched on the barrel of my gun, peering straight into my eyes. I flinched for a moment. Then it flew off and calmly landed on the ground. I pulled the trigger and it fell without a sound.

Now we were all really proud that ours was a guaranteed crow-free colony. Children would go out of the house with food without fearing them. We could dry curd-chillies and crisps without hanging up crow-feathers to scare them away. We heard the sounds of only the nice birds.

But last night, I did catch the sound of a crow cawing. At first, I thought I was imagining things. But soon I felt that the caw flew in mysteriously from somewhere and coiled around me. I checked every room. The sound fell suddenly. When I went over to shut the window, the darkness outside loomed like an enormous crow with its wings open for flight. It stared at me unwaveringly. I picked up my gun and fired a couple of shots. The neighbours heard and came running.

'The crows may come yet, be alert,' I told them and they nodded.

I must teach the residents how to shoot the crows. I always wanted to be a hunter.

Blue Film

Kumaran was still lazing in bed, pulling out the dagger from under the pillow and admiring its fine glint, cursing himself for being so dumb all this while, and imagining the scene of Paulochan falling dead at a single stab, when the sound that rose high above that Sunday's silence made him sit up. And there went a champion out of the camp of the Philistines, named Goliath, of Gath, whose height was six cubits and a span. And he had a helmet of brass on his head, and he was armed with a coat of mail; and the weight of the coat was brass worth five thousand shekels.

As the description of Goliath continued to flow out of the church's loudspeaker, mounted tediously on a gangly pole, in tired, phlegm-specked words, Kumaran, who was following the story with eyes falling shut due to sheer fatigue from the harsh noon sun and last night's sleeplessness, strayed from it and began to seek where life resided in the many highs and lows on the terrain of Paulochan's huge body with its cavernous mouth that slobbered like an infant's, the out-of-line teeth jutting out, and the eyeball-like black mole next to his nose. He heard Goliath snarl: 'Am I a dog, that thou comest to me with staves?'

Kumaran woke up fully and examined the dagger again. Its face was marked with lime. Amma had given it to him. 'Nothing like iron to ward off evil,' she had said. 'It is also to remember Grandpa by.' It was now just a toy made of iron, taken over by the brownish tinge of rust, having lost all of a well-wrought iron-blade's supple grace.

He pressed his thumb on that modest tool which the whitish lime scars had turned ungainly: a weakling. But Paulochan—he was strong enough to fell a champion. If this poor chap faltered even a little bit, if he missed the target even by a hair's breath, if he had to struggle to penetrate the skin—alas, that would be the end of him, sighed Kumaran.

Even as his depression deepened, Kumaran fervently wished he had a pistol. If he had one, he wouldn't be trying this crude method so highly prone to failure. He would have set up for Paulochan a nice and pretty death-hour.

The game would start when Paulochan would be waiting downstairs, calling out to him for last night's collection and, as per their daily ritual, showering abuse. Opening the door just a crack and peeping out from upstairs, Kumaran would catch a glimpse of him standing below. His face would be all ruddy with annoyance because no one would have answered his shouting. His lips would be quivering. Even the eagle-wing-coloured roots that showed beneath his faux-black hair would be quivering. *Crouch quietly in the room, do not make a sound or open the door—and he'll bound up, the wooden stairs shaking below him. When he reaches the landing, the door will be opened and the words will emerge: Please do not be angry. I have been waiting for thee.*

Paulochan will surely be taken aback. Paying no attention to the suspicion on his face, the doors and windows will be opened wide, and he will be invited in. Looking deep into his eyes now bulging with surprise at the gaily-coloured decorations that adorn the ceiling and the walls of the room, one would say in the mildest tone: This is for you. Surely that will be an auspicious start.

Taking advantage of his astonishment at the grandeur of the feast set up on the small, square table-top, the wine will be poured. The greedy boozer will gobble down the food and drink. I'll start chit-chatting, with the small freedom of being the host. Will keep filling his glass all the while. Will caress his cheeks fondly. When he starts tottering in his drunkenness, I will gently close the door. Then shut the windows. Will hold his head now nearly drooping off his neck in my left hand. Praying for an easy end, I will press the cold barrel of the gun on that head of hair that has been turned obscene with all those colours.

Before the trigger of the gun could be pressed, the sound of his name—'Kumaraa …!'—fell like a wave crashing. Kumaran fell down as the knots of his conspiracy came undone, and then helplessly peeped through the crack of the open door. Paulo's driver Muthu was standing downstairs. Paulochan can even read my mind, he thought, shivering. Quickly hiding the dagger under his pillow, he went and huddled next to the cot.

As his breathing grew strained from fear, and sweat spread its branches all over his body, Kumaran heard the sound of the old wooden stairs creaking contemptuously over that of his pounding heart. He sat, with all the powerlessness of a victim, flinging the door wide open instead of waiting for Muthu to break it down with a single kick and crush him. But all he heard was Muthu's voice from the stairs. A brief sentence in Tamil-ish Malayalam, that he was to take the film-crate to Menaka for the evening show there. He had gone away after throwing that short instruction at him. Kumaran got up and stood rooted to the spot for quite a while afterwards. He then shut the door, lay down on the cot, and began to sob into the pillow.

At Menaka, Sugunan took large puffs on his cigarette, and blew out the smoke into the excited faces surrounding him.

'Paulochan Muthalaali always brings this stuff here first, he does. I'd told him way back: "This girl's going to kill it."'

He gestured with his eyes a question—'how's it doing,' and answered it himself—'yes, fabulously!' And then, he laughed out loud, pleased with his successful foretelling.

Then, passing his eyes over each face, he whispered, 'That duffer Kumaran, he thought this is the old *Jeevitanauka*! Anyone would think that—that's the hush-hush ...'

A neck stretched out, breaking the circle of faces around Sugunan and asking: 'What hush-hush?'

Sugunan stirred again and said, 'That's what's written in pumpkin-sized letters on the crate—JEEVITANAUKA. Kumaran knew only when I told him. This movie's called *Miss Rani*.

One of the men gasped. 'Chetta, how's the story?'

Sugunan let his gaze wander over all the faces, cut an interval drawing a long breath, and inserting a sliver of silence, he gathered his voice together and began to thread a story into the ears now anchored inextricably in the deep of curiosity.

Rani, an exquisite beauty from the brothel run by the middle-aged Devaki. A budding dazzler. Pure-gold complexion. Big eyes. Tresses falling beyond her knees. Sexy body hair at her ankles. Breasts like lotus buds.

Moans and groans from the listeners formed brief interruptions, and then, the story continued.

Penniless chaps, cross-eyed fellows, cripples, droolers ... men of many kinds gathered at Devaki's doorstep to catch a glimpse of the peerless blossom. Devaki would holler, 'Leave you dogs!', and they would shuffle off. All but one drooler, who pretended that Devaki's cusswords were not meant for him. He hung around her window, praying for a glimpse of Rani's shadow, if nothing else. Finding cusswords ineffective, Devaki would then flash her goods at him and heap choicest abuses on his mother. He would return, utterly fulfilled. Our beauty would smile, watching the whole drama.

Time went by and one day, an aged merchant visited Devaki. Rani, adept in dance and music, pleasured him well (Sugunan described the pleasures through many facial and physical gestures, as well as animal-like grunts). The merchant who had come to spend the night fell hopelessly for the girl and stayed on. And then, he took off with her.

'And then?' one of the listeners asked with unbearable curiosity.

Sugunan's mouth curved in an obscene grimace. 'The rest is on the silver screen.'

Kumaran sat up at the eight o'clock siren. He sat still in the awareness of being the world's weakest man. He changed, and not wanting to see his teary eyes in the mirror, he shut the door and climbed down the stairs carefully, carrying *Jeevitanauka* on his shoulders.

Is a man allowed to kill another? If you murder your boss, will your troubles end? If a poor, helpless, lone man, whose relentlessly cruel boss denies him a decent wage for his labours, decides to react, would it be fair to condemn it as evil and immoral? Is it not cowardice to keep waiting endlessly for the fruit of generosity to ripen?

If your adversary is canny enough to read even your thoughts, then what hope is left? Torn by such questions and sobbing to God about his crippling fear, Kumaran was walking towards Menaka through an ill-lit bylane, when he heard a female voice. 'It's very heavy, isn't it?' He turned around, startled. Nothing could be seen, except a bandicoot scurrying behind the bushes.

Kumaran had taken a few more steps, when he heard the voice again. 'Can't you sit here for a bit? There's still some time before you reach Menaka.' Kumaran was petrified with fear. Just then a falling leaf brushed past his nose and he screamed. 'You scaredy-cat!' the voice teased him.

He put the crate down and stood frozen in terror. The voice pleaded, 'I am here, inside the crate. If you open the lid, I too will get some fresh air.' That frail old dagger could have saved me now even if it couldn't kill Paulochan, he thought. But the voice sounded piteous as it begged, 'Don't be scared, I won't harm you.' And so, he didn't think any further and opened *Jeevitanauka's* lid.

A thin girl with a wan look emerged out of the iron box. She took Kumaran's hand, walked towards a rock nearby, and sat down on it. She wiped the sweat on his brow with her saree, chided him for his unkempt beard, crumpled clothes and messy hair. But Kumaran was still frightened, and so he stood up. She caught his hand again and gently seated him next to herself. 'If you get so scared, you'll run a fever,' she mocked.

He could not bring himself to look at her face. She was admonishing him for not going home to visit his ailing mother, and was fussing over his dirty, untrimmed nails. Finally, gathering all the courage he could, Kumaran asked, 'Who are you?'

Pressing the weight of her whole body on his hand, she wept. Her sorrow beamed like sunrays coming out in the middle of a terrible downpour. 'I have lived with you for so long, but you still don't know me. Did you ever care to see me? How eagerly I sought you among the viewers every day. But it's also true that I did not wish to see you as I searched among the crowd of faces, all looking the same in the darkness of the theatre. I did not want to stay away from you even for a second. And now ...' A torrent rose from the depth of her eyes to cut her off in mid-sentence.

Seeing her break down like a child, he asked her innocently, 'Are you mad?'

'Yes,' she mumbled between her tears. 'Wasn't I crazy to love someone like you? And what about wanting to shoot Paulo if you had a gun, and then brooding over its rightness and wrongness—is that not madness?' She wept aloud.

Kumaran's eyes filled with darkness. He felt faint. The fear of being caught immobilized him. Grabbing his hands, she continued amidst her tears: 'I won't tell anyone. Trust me. I never wanted to scare you, even for fun. When you said you didn't know who I was, it broke my heart. I cried. Is it a crime to weep? If it is, then it's a crime worth committing. How long has it been since I cried like this. Please forgive me. How are you to love me when you have never even seen me. I am a fool. I know only the things that a fool would blurt out. Maybe I am insane. That's why I saw you alight on the tip of the blunt old dagger as a butterfly does on a flower. Why didn't I see a victim's blood or flesh? The barrel of the gun that crouched behind the bush when I was a fawn; the nets with a thousand eyes, like a broad-winged crane, in the water when I was a fish—how could I have forgotten those? Why do I not thirst for revenge, simmer in anger and hate? I know only this: I love you. The woman who loves in the shadows is like a tragic yakshi, clad in white and pining over unrequited love. Unable to touch the one she loves, never knowing his scent, she is the untiring eye that follows him, him alone. You were a ship with no travellers. And I, an albatross that criss-crossed the skies above, not pausing by your sails even once. Look, the queue in front of Menaka grows longer and longer in its greed to gulp down yet another prey. Please hold me close, just once. At least for tonight, shield me from those eyes.'

Is this story titled 'Blue Film' ending here? So Kumaran isn't holding her close? Maybe shifting into the darkness ... something further ...? Didn't Sugunan say that she was well-skilled in the art of love? If a story of this kind ends here without even the promise of to-be-continued-next-week, what'll happen to readers like us, who're waiting to slurp the story down their big slobbering mouths?

Householder

This isn't a city or town or something. There are big buildings, narrow lanes, many cars and stuff, and some human beings here. This place started out from the back-of-beyond, but hasn't reached anywhere yet. In two distinct corners of this place, north and south, in the same year, on the same day, were born two men. Their parents gave them the same name: Krishnan. These two Krishnans have never met. Their parents haven't met either. Except for their name, there is nothing that connects them. One of the Krishnans is a big, burly man. The other one is pint-sized.

Krishnan Big wakes up early every day. Krishnan Little wakes up late. But today was the day of Vavu Bali, on which we offer food to our loved ones who have departed, and because he had to perform the ritual, Krishnan Little woke up early, like Krishnan Big. Till two years back, his father used to make the offering. After his death, the task fell on Krishnan Little on Amma's insistence.

Krishnan Little stepped out from his house. The road was dark, and filled with people and vehicles. Everyone was on their way to make offerings, it seemed. Krishnan Little walked towards the south. His father used to believe that for the ritual to be effective, you had to walk right up to the sea and make the offering. Amma thought the same, so Krishnan Little really did have to walk all the way there.

People milled about in the lane leading to the seashore. Krishnan Little paused, taking in the crowd and the bustle. After some time, he headed towards the road opposite the lane. There was very little light there. And fewer people. He walked for a while and then came across a modest little house in the midst of two-storey mansions. It had a wall that was decidedly unglamorous compared to those of the stately homes surrounding it; the lime plaster was peeling off. The heads of the gates were bound together closely with copper wire. However, since the bodies of the gates did not share the closeness of their heads, there was a gap in the middle; so big was this gap that a person could slip in or out easily. All over the compound, trees and plants grew furious and free. As he stood staring at the house for some time, Krishnan Little thought about going in there for a bit. Someone entering a house so early in the day, when it was still so dark—that might disturb the people living there somewhat. So the first thing they'd most likely ask would be: Who are you? Better to reveal one's real name: Krishnan. What do you want, would be the next question. What answer could he offer to that, he thought for a second. What's wrong with telling the truth? I'll tell the truth. I was at the seashore for the *bali*. I came this way because I found it very distasteful. They may then ask: Why didn't you offer the bali? My father, his father, all the patriarchs of the family, all of them were a plague on not just human beings but on everything alive and existing. Last year, Amma came along, and so I couldn't sneak away. This year she stayed back. If this makes them angry and makes them ask me to leave, I just will.

Krishnan Big did not know that the other Krishnan, born on the same day same year same time as him, was curious about his house, and had walked into his compound, and was, right then, peering at him from outside the kitchen window. He had, as usual, wrapped a towel around his waist and begun his day reciting poetry:

> *Flowered on time, in season, and yet,*
> *never did it happen,*
> *My Blossoming.*
> *Maybe the day I burn*
> *brilliant in a blazing fire*
> *My flowers will find form*
> *And finally bloom.*

The towel around Krishnan Big's potbelly looked like it would drop any time. He was wiping off the sweat trickling down his bald head to his forehead. His mind was immersed in poetry as he measured the rice out and walked about the kitchen. As he washed the rice, he continued to recite:

Kindly Death, big brother of Sleep,
How I wish you'd creep up quietly,
Clap your palms around my eyes,
when I sat enraptured in a beloved poem.

Krishnan Little wondered: What is he washing, the rice or the line?

Krishnan Big put the rice into the pot and lit the fire. He was in the habit of walking ceaselessly from one poem to another, like you walk in a rice field, from one mud-path to another.

Death spoke in kindly tones
'Leave aside the world, arise, it's time
Allow me to snuff out the lamp.'

The rice was boiling, when he took a coconut from one side of the hearth and broke it. He drank up the coconut water, and it soaked the line 'My gait, my feeling ...' Krishnan Big wiped his lips dry and recited:

Did my desire to feel
Make my steps languid?
Death turned, crying,
'What! Forsake me thus?
Your cheeks are flushed
Your eyes glint so
Your heart is pounding,
You live!

Krishnan Little knew what he would do next. He'll grind the coconut to a chammandi-paste. Maybe make another curry. Or pour some curd, or heat up some leftovers from last night. He wasn't mistaken. Krishnan Big scraped out the coconut flesh and went to the grinding-stone in the pantry outside the kitchen. Krishnan Little peered into the adjacent room. A shelf full of books. Unwashed shirts hanging from pegs on the wall. The floor littered with magazines still in their postal packaging. A rusty bicycle in a corner. Pencil sketches of two cats. An easy chair. There are no women here, Krishnan Little felt certain. If there were, the house would have been more neat and orderly. Maybe there had been a woman here. Maybe she left because she couldn't put up with someone like him. Or maybe he is unmarried—Krishnan Little corrected himself. Why was he still unmarried? A number of doubts assailed Krishnan Little in a very short while.

Krishnan Big ground the chammandi without a clue, all this while, that someone was standing outside his house riddled by so many questions. He prepared the vegetables for an avial. The rice was cooked and he drained it. He put the chinachatti on the hearth to fry mustard to temper the buttermilk. As he fried it, Krishnan Big stumbled after the line 'Drunk from fitting a letter or two ...', and struggled to move beyond, repeating it again and again. He couldn't cross into the next.

As he stayed stuck on the same line, the mustard burned. Krishnan Little's jaw ached to tell him to look at the frying pan, but he held back. Quite oblivious to the mustard's fate, Krishnan Big got up and went into the other room. In the blink of an eye, he had pulled out a little book from the shelf, taken a look inside, and replaced it.

> *Drunk from fitting a letter or two,*
> *Impatient for fame, we, pretend-poets*
> *Ah, if only we would learn modesty*
> *From those of long ago, those who*
> *made knowledge their vow.*

Who is this big man, and whose poetry is he reciting from memory—many such questions began to gather in Krishnan Little's mind. Maybe he could ask all these questions. Maybe he could also apologize for having lurked there so long. But what if this man who lived here alone with just books for company lost his temper? What if he swung that big hand of his? The thought of these possible consequences made Krishnan Little abandon the plan.

Krishnan Big returned to the kitchen and ladled the rice onto a big plate. He spooned the avial and the buttermilk into two small bowls. From a glass jar, he took out some tender mango-in-mustard pickle. As he saw this and as the scent of the food encircled him, Krishnan Little felt his mouth water. He had fasted last evening and eaten little during the day. Krishnan Big arranged the dishes on the floor, sat down cross-legged, and poured the buttermilk into the hot rice. He then spooned a bit of the tender mango pickle on top. He was going to enjoy every morsel. That's how he grew so big, thought Krishnan Little—from eating rice like this for breakfast, lunch and dinner. Meanwhile, Krishnan Big was making balls out of the rice, and reciting poetry as though he were caressing and coddling them.

> *Hey dark girl of toil and sweat,*
> *Who made you so adept at love?*
> *Who mixed sweet honey in your voice?*
> *Who touched your feathers with fragrance?*
> *Who made the lotus bloom and rise,*
> *from within that sultry flesh?*

The balls of rice filled the plate. Krishnan Big did not eat a single one. Krishnan Little remembered how Amma used to say, that cooking a meal killed your appetite. Maybe this big man also felt so. Or is he waiting for someone to share the meal with? Who is going to come so early this morning? From his activities, it seemed that he was unlikely to have friends or relatives. Krishnan Little felt overwhelmed by his curiosity. It was also starting to get light outside. Surely, if any neighbour spotted a strange man slinking near the kitchen-window, there would be trouble. Krishnan Little really wanted to ask all his questions at once. But he was also afraid. Still, he decided to ask and opened his mouth to do so. But right then, Krishnan Big got up. That gave Krishnan Little a fright. Krishnan Big stepped out into the pantry. The other Krishnan was now alert—is he coming this way? But he couldn't hear footsteps approach. There was the sound of water falling, and above it, of poetry.

> *In that last drop of life in which*
> *my wakeful brain murmurs,*
> *in the island amidst ocean's vastness,*
> *in the last throbbing star of a wasted universe,*
> *You will be with me, as the moment of*
> *our last kiss flashes by,*
> *And then in your eye I will see, the beauty*
> *of the truth, that embraces Life and Death.*

Krishnan Big had returned after washing his hands. Does this man eat poetry for his meals? If so, why did he cook all this rice and curry? Or is he mentally disturbed? If not, why does he behave so strangely? As Krishnan Little lingered there, thinking that this was the first time he had encountered such a strange situation, Krishnan Big stopped reciting poetry. Why did he stop? Maybe someone was coming ...? Krishnan Little was asking himself that question, when Krishnan Big glanced outside through the kitchen door and smiled. That gave Krishnan Little a fright, and he decided to leave. But before he could move away soundlessly, the curiosity about who the visitor might be gripped him. He peeped inside, feeling quite nervous. Seeing the guest who had come in, as quietly as a dry leaf falling on the ground, Krishnan Little was totally confounded. Good God, who was this? What was happening?

Krishnan Big received his guest lovingly and respectfully. Seeing the guest look around, head tilted, fully alert and keen-eyed, Krishnan Little crouched behind the kitchen window-pane for fear of being spotted.

The guest went into the inner room and took a look at all the books. The poetry of Vallathol Narayana Menon seemed to get the most attention. After touching the dried-up ink-pot, walking around the bicycle, and hanging around the inner room for some more time, the guest returned to the kitchen and began to eat the balls of rice with great relish.

Were they talking? Or was he just imagining it? No, he wasn't. If he were imagining it, why would Krishnan Big shake his head so? Krishnan Little was so stumped, he began to shiver.

Krishnan Big's guest finished his meal and went out into the garden, looking at the plants with great interest. Clearly pleased that they were growing fast and abundantly, he cocked his head and turned to Krishnan Big. A squirrel on the branch of a mango tree said something then, as though he were an acquaintance, and the guest bounded up there in a single step. Then onto the tamarind tree, and then the jackfruit tree, and finally, towards the sky.

Krishnan Little followed Krishnan Big's upward glance. He saw a dot of black soaring up as though to touch the sky. Was it possible for a bird to fly so high? Krishnan Little was really wonderstruck.

Krishnan Big in the story is, without a doubt, Malayalam's beloved poet, Vailoppily Sreedhara Menon (1911–1985). He lived a solitary life, immersed in poetry, and was believed to have friends in the animal world, especially crows.

The Grievance

Somebody grabbed Radha's buttocks when she was getting off the bus. She screamed, turned around sharply, only to see a fair-skinned, tall fellow with a pinched face shove aside the other passengers and make his way towards the back door. Radha pushed aside the other women near the door in the front, jumped out, and ran towards the back door. But by then, he had crossed the road and disappeared into a bylane.

When she returned, Sumathy was waiting at the bus-stop.

'Where did you go?'

Radha looked sullen.

'What's with the teary eyes?'

'Someone grabbed me.'

'And?'

'It hurts.'

'Didn't you beat up the mangy dog?'

'No, before I could get my hands on him, he ran off.'

'Did you recognize him?'

'One of the chaps who sells vegetables in the market.'

Radha and Sumathy worked in a textile shop on Kottayam's K. K. Road. When they got off every morning at the Baker Junction and walk to the shop, Radha would be chattering on and on. Sumathy would giggle, and that would set Radha off again. Sometimes, the tales wouldn't end even when they had reached the shop. That would make the manager, a Tamilian, roll his eyes. Radha and Sumathy would pretend to be scared.

That day, they had got past P. T. Chacko's statue and the YMCA; Radha hadn't uttered a word. So Sumathy asked, 'Why, what happened? No news today?'

Radha did not reply.

The shop opened and before long, a family from Ponkunnam came to get a wedding trousseau. Radha pulled out a couple of sarees. Sumathy noticed that she was listless; she wasn't unfolding the sarees for the customers to see, or making an effort to pick sarees that would complement the bride's complexion. 'I'll handle this,' she told Radha, directing her back to her seat. 'You go and cut two metres of the coarse-cloth.'

Seeing Radha cut three metres instead of two, and pack a 40-inch bra instead of 32, the senior supervisor, Valsamma, asked Sumathy, 'What's wrong with her?'

'Awful headache since morning,' said Sumathy.

'Hmm ...' Valsamma didn't sound convinced.

When Radha didn't turn up while they were eating lunch, Valsamma asked Sumathy again, 'Where is she?'

'She was coming this way,' Sumathy replied, struggling to open her tiffin-box.

'Try opening it with a crowbar …?' Sulfat laughed at Sumathy—and said, 'Radha's been sitting in the godown.'

Seeing her all alone amidst the big bundles of cloth, Sumathy asked, 'Why're you sitting here?'

'Just …'

'Not having lunch?'

'No.'

'Why?'

'I'll have no peace till I give him a tight slap.'

'Ah, that! Just that?' Sumathy laughed. 'Come here, won't you?'

Radha and Sumathy stepped out of the shop and walked towards the market.

'Let's go look at the market junction. He usually parks his cart there.'

They couldn't find him there.

'Where do we look now?' Sumathy asked.

'Near the Indian Coffee House, inside the market.'

They hung around the coffee house for some time. He was not to be seen.

'Shall we ask someone?'

Yes, nodded Sumathy.

Radha went up to a shirt-less betel-leaf seller who was announcing his wares loudly. 'Hey, chetta, did you see the guy who sells vegetables here? Tall, fair-ish, gaunt face? Do you know him?'

He spat out the betel-leaf in his mouth, and then asked, 'Bennichan, maybe?'

Hearing that name, a laugh rang out and placed itself right in front of the betel-leaf seller. Radha and Sumathy looked at it, surprised. The owner of that laugh was an old lady selling ginger nearby.

'My dearies, this fellow Benni, is just about as tall as this pen-knife!' she said and began to laugh again. Radha and Sumathy began to feel somewhat lost. Then she asked, 'Hey girls, do you know where he comes from?'

'Our house is in Kudamaloor,' Sumathy said. 'He takes the bus that comes that way?'

'Ah, then that's our guy Rameshan.'

The old lady did not like the betel-seller piping up, pleased with himself at having found the answer first. She spat hard at the answer and pointed to the left.

'See, that's his cart.'

Radha and Sumathy hurried to the cart. A young fellow, fifteen or sixteen years of age, stood minding it.

'Where's Rameshan?' Radha asked.

The boy looked at them suspiciously. 'There,' he pointed. 'He's over there. Just go inside the lane and turn left.'

When they turned into the lane, the hesitation in the boy's eyes overtook them and warned: 'Should you ...? They're probably all sloshed and wasted ...'

The lane ended in a row of toilets. On the steps, there were a few men, sitting and drinking. Sumathy looked at

Radha, uncertainly. Radha strode ahead and Sumathy followed.

'Is any of you the vegetable seller Rameshan?'

None of them replied. They were all busy filling empty glasses, and continued to talk amongst themselves.

Radha made one more attempt. 'Did a chap named Rameshan come around here?'

One of the older men with a red towel around his head called out without taking his eyes off the glass he was pouring into: 'Who's shitting in there? Rameshan?'

'No, me—Benny,' came a voice from inside one of the toilets.

'You're looking upset since you returned from work,' Amma said to Radha.

'It's nothing,' said Radha.

'For heaven's sake, just spit it out! What happened?'

'I fell down while getting off the bus.'

'Show me, where?'

Radha was lying in bed face down. Amma checked.

'Gosh, it's become stone-hard,' she said and stood up.

'Where are you going?' asked Radha.

'You lie down. I'll go get some oil to soothe the bruise.'

From her cot, Radha could hear the leaves in the yard chattering away as Amma went off hurriedly to the neighbour's.

'Chechi,' asked the next-door neighbour Maniamma, 'what's up with Radha?'

'Oh, she just fell down while getting off the bus.'

'Tell her to walk properly, not skip and hop,' Maniamma poured out the oil and with it, some advice.

As Amma began to massage in the oil, she said in a rather low voice, 'This doesn't look like a bruise from a fall ... more like someone gave you a tight slap ...'

Radha leapt up at that, and Amma quickly escaped on the pretext of her evening prayer.

'Check if he's on the bus,' Radha reminded Sumathy while they waited at the stop.

'Sure,' said Sumathy. 'We must thump him right inside the bus.'

The bus arrived with the usual crowding inside. Radha and Sumathy didn't hurry; they waited, watching the men's line closely. They got in, but instead of moving up to the front, they hung back on the sides, watching each male face through every little space that opened up in the crowd.

'Is he here?' Sumathy asked in a whisper.

'I think, no,' Radha whispered back.

As soon as the bus stopped at Baker Junction, Radha clambered out quickly and rushed towards the men's door. Everyone got out, but there was no sign of Rameshan.

'What do we do now?'

'Let's go to the market. Maybe he took another bus today.'

They didn't find anyone near his cart.

Where's that young boy who was here yesterday, they were thinking, when someone called out to them from the back. They turned around and found him on the second storey of the coffee house, drinking coffee.

'He didn't come here yesterday,' he told them. 'He dives deep now and then. Takes time to come up again.'

'Will he come today?'

'Can't say.'

'Tell us where he lives …?'

'What for?'

'To invite him to my wedding.' That was Radha.

His face brightened up. 'You know Panambaalam?'

Radha nodded.

'Get off there and walk to the Thonnaguzhi school. Ask anyone there and they will show you the way.'

That day, they got out of the shop earlier.

When they were walking from Panambaalam to the Thonnaguzhi school, Sumathy remembered going to the temple at Kolott with her mother.

'There used to be a swami there,' she said, going back a few years. 'Amma would listen only to him.'

'He had a flunky, a guy called Chacko. This swami, he used to get Chacko to make some statuettes—Ganapati,

Siva. Clumsy he was! But the swami was all fired up about him.'

'You're going to jabber on and we'll miss the school!'

'Oh, really! As if I don't know the roads here. Keep walking, it's a long way from here.'

When they stopped beside the Thonnaguzhy school, they didn't see anyone around; except a little girl playing outside a house just opposite. Radha went up to boundary wall and asked, 'Molé, do you know where this chap Rameshan lives? He sells vegetables.'

The girl ran inside calling out to her mother, and came back at the same speed with her.

'Over there, on the road going downhill ... the first house,' the woman said, pointing to a lane next to the school. 'Be careful ... the road is slippery.'

It was a steep slope. They stepped gingerly, holding each other's hand, and stopped before the first house. It was small, and fenced with some hibiscus trees and other shrubs. In the tiny yard, some coconut tree spathes and branches had been left to dry. A broken plastic chair lay in the middle. The steps from the lane into the yard were broken.

When they stepped into the yard, a woman came out, holding a baby on her hip. She had probably been nursing it; the hooks on her blouse were all undone and her breasts looked ready to leap out any moment.

'Who are you?' she asked.

'We're here to see Rameshan,' Radha answered.

'Chettan is not at home.'

'When will he be back?'

'You didn't tell me who you are.'

'We need to see him.'

'What for?'

'That we can tell only him.'

'I am his wife. What is it you have to tell him that *I* shouldn't know?'

'You don't have to know, for the time being,' Sumathy pushed Radha aside and moved forward. 'It's a nasty business.'

'What nasty business, you little shrew? What's the shit you are going to tell my man?'

'Oh, yes! Your man's a piece of shit. That's what!'

'Phhbha!' the woman spat hard. 'What's so shitty about my man, you born-of-a-whore-no-good?'

Laying the infant down on the veranda, the woman tightened her lungi and began to charge at Sumathy.

'He grabbed this girl's bum!'

'If you swing your bums before men, any man'd grab them! Nothing to raise hell about!'

This time Radha pushed Sumathy aside and sprang up, spitting really hard. 'Phhabhha! So shove your mother in front so that he can grab her bum too, you bitch!'

The neighbours came out, and an old lady made Rameshan's wife go back into the house. Some other women from the houses nearby gathered there. They had nothing to do, so they just hung about, chins in hand.

Radha and Sumathy stood there for a little while. When they turned to leave, they could hear Rameshan's wife wailing.

They reached the market early. They waited, but Rameshan did not turn up. After a while, the boy who they had talked to the other day came up.

'Did you meet Chettan?'

'No.'

'Today he'll come to the goods shed for sure. That's where everyone pays the interest. Just go there.'

They took an autorickshaw.

'Radhamani chechi called me yesterday—our Manager-Annaachi thinks we are really shirking at work.'

'You go to the shop if you want,' said Radha. 'I can go by myself.'

They waited under a tree near the goods shed, covering their faces with the hems of their sarees; dust came faster than the trains.

'Maybe the boy fooled us. Maybe he won't come here ...?'

'Let's see,' said Radha.

A couple of trains passed, rushing in different directions. Sumathy called the shop manager to tell him they wouldn't be working that day. The dust made Radha sneeze endlessly.

Seeing someone cross the railway tracks and step on the road, Sumathy asked, 'Look, is that our man?'

Radha looked carefully, and then without replying, bounded towards him. But before she reached, a speeding autorickshaw screeched up and stopped a hair's breadth away, almost knocking her down. Her foot slipped off the pavement. Red shone on the sharp things that were jutting out of the auto. And then, with a roar, the auto spat smoke on the now prone Rameshan's face, and tore down the road, turning into a bylane.

Sumathy ran towards Radha, who was petrified with fear. The din of vehicles rushing off, too scared to stop, rose above Rameshan's slurring tones. The thick consonants of a goods train running southwards swallowed all other sounds as it stretched further and further to the south.

Radha stepped into the middle of the road, in front of a car, and looked at the driver. Sumathy and she couldn't make out if he was sympathetic to them or if it was just trepidation, if it was out of fear for himself or from concern for a man's desperate plea to save his life, but he drove fast.

When they left the hospital, they were silent.

After some time, Radha said, 'Fellows like him deserve no sympathy, really.'

'Then why did you cart him here to the hospital?' Sumathy sounded irritated.

'What else should one do when some fellow's lying on his back, dying on the road?'

Sumathy thought for a moment and agreed with her.

'Umm, and there's something else.'

Sumathy looked at Radha, asking, what else.

'If he dies, how will I slap him?'

'Yes, absolutely,' said Sumathy, laughing.

After a week, Radha asked Sumathy, 'Why don't we go to the hospital?

'Why?' Sumathy asked. It didn't seem necessary.

'He must have recovered by now.'

'You mean?'

'He's going to learn a lesson only when we give him a dose of verbal shit, and a few slaps.'

Sumathy agreed.

They went to the hospital, but the head nurse told them that Rameshan's relatives had taken him to some other hospital that very day.

They looked for him in the district hospital, and some private hospitals too. They did find a Rameshan who had been hacked. But that was a toddy-tapper from Neendur.

'What do we do now?' Sumathy asked.

'Let's go back to that boy and find out?'

'Let's not. We could land in trouble.'

'Then what?'

Sumathy thought for a while and said, 'Why don't we go to his house again after a few days?'

'And?'

'Just give him a good slap right there.'

Radha was quiet, thinking.

'What? Are you afraid of him?'

'No. But when I take aim, that wife of his is going to jump in the middle.'

'So what? Give her a tight one too!'

One evening, when the air had cooled down, they left the shop.

'You two are taking it really easy,' their Tamilian boss complained. 'At this rate, you are going to be fired,' he threatened.

'Just one more day,' Sumathy pleaded.

When they reached the slope just above Rameshan's house, an old man was making his way up carefully, leaning on his walking-stick. The lane was very narrow, so they waited for him to come up.

By the time he reached the top of the slope, he was panting, and so exhausted that he nearly fell. Radha and Sumathy grabbed his arms and helped him sit down on a rock nearby. He dropped his stick as soon as he sat, and took a deep breath, pushing down his hitched-up mundu between his legs. After he had caught his breath, he looked up and smiled gratefully.

When Radha and Sumathy turned to leave, he asked, 'Where are you going? There's been a death. Are you going there?'

'No, to Rameshan's,' Sumathy said.

'That's what I asked. The sanchayanam got over today.'

Sumathy looked at Radha. The old man drew in a big breath through his mouth.

On their way back, they did not feel like talking. But after some time, Sumathy asked, 'Do you feel sad that you couldn't whack him?'

Radha didn't say anything.

After some time, she asked, 'Do *you* feel sad?'

Sumathy didn't say anything either.

Travelling Together

'How should we die?' Radhamani asked Sumathy.

'On the railway tracks.'

'But …' Radhamani hesitated, 'what if the train throws us to two sides?'

That's true, thought Sumathy. We might be thrown apart, on either side of the tracks. Better not try. At least in death, we must lie together.

'Let's drown in the river,' Sumathy suggested.

'But I can swim,' Radhamani sounded despondent.

'What if we consume poison?' A glimmer of hope shone in Sumathy's voice.

'Some stuff just burns your throat,' Sumathy looked sadly at Radhamani.

'I am angry with God.'

'Why?'

'No idea! Just angry!'

Radhamani wanted to hug Sumathy and give her a kiss. She threw a stealthy glance around and clasped her hand.

'What are we going to do after we die?'

'No idea.'

'But it will be better than this.'

'We should go to a studio and get a photo of us hugging before we die,' Radhamani said and smiled.

When the photographer was getting the lights ready, Sumathy said, 'Let's hug.'

She put her hand around Radhamani's shoulder and hugged her close.

The photographer was piqued. 'Cchhi! What's this, girls? Move apart. A tiny bit, now.'

He pushed them apart and set the lights on their faces.

'Now smile.'

They didn't.

'Smile,' he repeated.

They still did not smile.

'It will look awful if you don't smile,' he warned.

'We will come back when we can smile,' said Radhamani and Sumathy. Clasping their hands together, they left the studio, walking past the pictures of newly-weds and wedding anniversaries.

Kamikakushi

1

True?

Yes, sir, true.

Did you see?

There's nothing left to be seen.

What do we do now?

That's what we are wondering too, master. Where did it all go?

You fools, question the people around there!

There's nobody there, sir.

Then?

Just two families lived there. In one, the husband, wife and three kids. In the other, an old woman and a man.

Interrogate them.

But they too have left the place, sir.

Didn't you suspect them?

Yes, sir.

Then how did they get away, you idiots? Get them down here, now!

Yes, sir.

2

Since when have you been living below the mountain?

Bee' ther' sinc' ah can remember.

Remember?

Wa' born ther'.

Where did you run off to from there last night?

Had no plan to run off anywher', masta.

Why did you leave?

Wer' helpl'ss.

Helpless?

No matte' who asks wha', we can't say a thin'. If we do, they take us insid' the forest an'...

So you *are* afraid?

Yes, masta.

What all did you take when you left?

Som' pots t' make gruel, som' clothes, som' rice and th'ngs.

Nothing else?

No, masta.

Is that the truth?

Yea, true.

The forest and the mountain there are missing since yesterday. Where did you spirit them away? Tell the truth! Do you know what the punishment for lying is?

Yea, y'r 'ighness.

Why are your beggar brats laughing?

We aren't laughin', masta.

Really, you miserable bums? Saying stupid things? Okay, who's laughing then?

The forest is laughing.

The mountain is laughing.

Vowel-Consonant

The Malayalam word for 'vowel', 'swaram', also means the deathless 'soul'. That for 'consonant', 'vyanjanam', refers to the 'mortal body'. It also means 'to mark'. Some breathe the fresh air of freedom, grow out of social moulds, and towards swaram. Others have only consonants. They can only see the flesh, regard others as mortal bodies that succumb to violence. Some, like Mustapha, grow, joining the consonant to the vowel.

Mustapha's Umma offered *subahi* prayers. Swept the yard. Cooked rice and curries. Washed the clothes. Took a bath. Combed her hair. Powdered her face. Draped a new sari. Kept the money to pay off the debt at the corner shop on top of the rice tin. Packed some essentials in a small bag. Sat down for some time, leaving her mind completely empty. She then shut the door behind her and stuffed a small note inside the bolt.

Mustapha did not feel any tears coming. He didn't feel hungry. He didn't hear anything that the stream of visitors was saying.

'Not eating dinner?' asked Bappa.

'No,' said Mustapha.

'Your sister, did she eat?'

Mustapha went and sat down close to his sister. Don't cry, he wanted to tell her, but didn't.

'When she's done crying, tell her to wash the dirty dishes,' Mustapha's father said, and let out a burp. Then he went out into the veranda and lit a beedi. It was dark outside. Mustapha stayed inside.

Next morning, Bappa went out as usual and hung around the roadside at the junction. Came home for lunch and had his siesta. Then went out again in the evening.

'I'll kill him, Chandra,' Mustapha said.

'How?' asked Chandran.

'No idea how.'

'Have you seen him?'

'No.'

'He's just about our age, but *verrr...y* strong. And capable of annny...thing. There are many police cases registered against him—four or five in our station alone.'

'But I still want to kill him!' Mustapha said, fighting back tears.

'They're the quarry mafia. So stay away. Everyone will forget this after a few days anyway,' Chandran tried to console him.

Two or three days passed. People spun newer and newer stories about Mustapha's mother. He could not sleep or eat any more.

'Chandra,' he said, 'I *have* to kill him.'

'Hey, you really can't, you know.'

'Come on, tell me how! Just one idea!'

Chandran began to think of ways, and Mustapha waited patiently till he found one.

'This sought of fellow can be finished off only if we pay someone else … a professional …' Chandran said at last, 'otherwise it is very risky.'

'That's fine.'

'It'll be very costly, though.'

'I'll pay.'

'But do you have any money?'

Mustapha nodded.

Chandra made some inquiries. His colleagues in the police services also helped. Many such professionals were lodged inside the jail. Some had left the field. In the end, he found someone who had recently been released.

'This guy's good,' said Chandran, as he shared the details, 'but hard to convince.'

Mustapha looked at the name and address.

The room was behind a closed bar. When Mustapha reached the place, the man was searching for a lost needle under the bed. Hearing Mustapha's footfall, he poked his head out from the darkness there and stared at him. Mustapha felt nervous. He then drew back into the darkness, and after a few minutes, emerged with a needle in hand. Mustapha stood waiting. The man didn't look at him; instead, he began to thread the needle. He kept missing the eye when he brought the tip of the thread close to it. He tried again, and again, and again. Finally, he managed to thread it. Then he pulled a shirt off the clothesline, yanked a button that hung from it like a loose tooth, and began to sew it back. Mustapha watched intently. Done with the sewing, the man put the shirt back and stuck the needle on the page of a wall-calendar. He then sat down on his bed. Why are you here, he gestured to Mustapha, raising his eyebrows.

'To have someone killed.'

'Right now?'

'As you wish.'

'Kill who?'

'Sura, who drives the tipper-lorry.'

'What for?'

'He took my Umma.'

'He took Umma or did Umma leave with him?'

Mustapha did not answer. He waited.

'Tell me!' he sounded louder.

Mustapha was still quiet.

'Where is your Umma now?'

Mustapha felt the tears coming, but did not let them fall.

'In his house,' he said.

'Didn't take her somewhere to sell?'

At this, Mustapha began to weep.

The man looked at Mustapha intently. Then he went over to the stove and poured kerosene into it. Pulled out the wick, put on it a pan of water, boiled it, and made coffee. He poured it into a glass and began to drink.

'I can pay,' Mustapha stopped sobbing and spoke.

'What's your line of trade?'

'Nothing in particular.'

'So where'll you find the money?'

'Umma left her gold chain and bangles behind. I'll sell them.'

'Who all do you have at home?'

'Bappa and sister.'

'What does Bappa do?'

'He doesn't work. My sister is in school. Class Ten.'

'How did you people get by with no one working?'

'Umma used to work in the rubber factory.'

He spat out the coffee dregs and slipped the glass under the bed. All this time, he kept looking at Mustapha.

'You can go now,' he said, pulling out the needle again from the calendar.

'I have no other way,' Mustapha begged with folded hands. 'I'm sick and tired of bowing my head all the time. My sister's quitting school. She might do something crazy to herself.'

He came close. Mustapha looked into his eyes, hoping to find a drop of pity.

'If you're so mad and sad, why not finish him off yourself?'

'Don't have the guts …'

'Then forget about it!'

He picked up another shirt and said, 'This is not a job one can do for a pittance. And I have sewing to finish, so leave.'

Mustapha went to Chandran again. Chandran told him to meet the man one more time. 'He'll call me names,' Mustapha was afraid. Chandran reassured him, and so he went again. But the man refused. Mustapha went many times. He kept refusing. One day when Mustapha went there again, the man was looking at his right thumb and frowning.

'Thumb nail's ingrowing,' Mustapha said in a low voice.

'I know.'

'Cut a lemon, dip it in salt, and press it there.'

The man looked up. Mustapha was looking at a corner of the room where lemons lay next to onions and potatoes.

'It'll sting first.'

'You don't hang around—leave.'

Then he fixed his gaze on the thumb and said, 'I have agreed to another job.'

Mustapha continued to wait. Then the man rose, picked up the lemon, cut it, and dipped it in salt.

'At least tell me how to kill a man,' Mustapha pleaded.

'That won't work.' The man pressed the lemon slice to his sore thumb. The stinging brought a grimace on his face. 'To carry it out smoothly, you've got to know the guy's nature, his movements, dwelling, habits, his connections … if you don't, it'll fail.'

'Sura's part of the quarry gang. Terribly strong!'

'Boy, you need two different knives to cut a leaf and iron.'

Mustapha didn't catch that.

Mustapha visited the next day too. The man was getting ready to go somewhere; Mustapha stood by quietly. The man was quiet too. He pulled out a piece of paper from beneath the mattress, crumpled it, and thrust it inside his rolled-up sleeve. Then he locked the room and put the key in a pouch at his waist. He paid Mustapha no attention, yet Mustapha followed him.

'Is that finger healing?'

He nodded.

'Onion juice and lime work well too,' Mustapha added.

An autorickshaw came up the road. He was climbing in when Mustapha asked, 'Can I come too?'

The man threw him a look that asked: For what? He was silent for a few moments and then said, 'Get in.'

They reached the railway station.

Sitting on the train, he asked Mustapha, 'How come you know such home remedies?'

'Umma taught me.'

'Where did she learn?'

'Her father was a vaidyan.' Mustapha pulled up the window of the compartment and said, 'For mumps, you have to get mud from a wasp's nest.'

He nodded. Mustapha looked through the window and thrust his arm out. It rose slowly in the speed and the wind.

'Sura always has two or three people around him,' he said, pulling it back in. 'Chandran says that he has a pistol on his hip all the time.'

The man was silent. The train reached a station. They got off and hailed an autorickshaw. Mustapha did not ask where they were going, nor did the man tell him. He kept pulling out the piece of paper from his sleeve and consulting it. Mustapha could spy map-lines, marking out some roads on it. The auto stopped in a very secluded, rural place. They got out. The man consulted his piece of paper again and began to walk.

'If anyone asks anything, I will be the one replying,' he said.

No one asked them anything. After walking a while on a reddish, sandstone path, he entered into an alley just wide enough for one person. He walked ahead and Mustapha followed. Before them wafted the sounds of clothes being beaten on washing-stones. The path ended in front of a flight of steps leading up to a house. Someone came running down towards them.

'Are you the ambulance people?'

Mustapha looked at the man, unsure. He was unmoved.

'You must be his readers, right?' asked the man who had come running. But he did not wait for a response, and shouted out to someone, 'They've come to see Sir. Take them up.'

An elderly woman came down from the small yard in front of the house.

'You go up. Let me check if the ambulance is here,' suggested the man and walked off.

The man and Mustapha stepped into the house.

'Sir is in that room,' the old woman pointed.

They went in. A small man, around sixty, lay on the bed, struggling hard for breath, his back arching in agony. He'll die right now, thought Mustapha. He stepped back, went out to another room and sat down there.

'No one else here?' He heard the man ask the old woman.

'Sir lives alone. Some people come to meet him now and then.'

'Who are these people?'

'I don't know all that.'

'Who're you to him?'

'I just come here to pick some wild arrowroot from his yard sometimes.'

'Not many neighbours, are there?'

'There are some to the southern side. There are paddy fields beyond the yard.'

Mustapha peeked out back. The backyard was filled with trees. There were many birds. The paddy fields could be seen through the leafy abundance.

After some time, the ambulance people came along with the man who had gone seeking them. They carried the sick man out.

'Please shut the windows and doors,' one of them called out.

The old woman shut the door and the windows.

When they were returning, the train was nearly empty. Mustapha and the man took seats opposite each other.

'The poor man, I hope he lives …' Mustapha said.

The man did not say anything.

'Couldn't bear to watch him struggle so hard for his life … that's why I jumped out so quick.'

The man still stayed silent. He kept looking outside the window.

'When I was a kid, I used to kill tadpoles. Umma used to say, if you do that my breasts will swell and become painful. So I stopped.'

The man then turned to look at Mustapha. His face seemed taut with fear.

'You know him? He used to write,' Mustapha asked.

He pretended to not have heard the question.

'Here, I took this from that room ...' Mustapha held out one of the writer's books. 'This had caused big trouble, remember? Was all over the papers ...'

The man looked at the photo of the writer on the back cover and sighed. 'Hope nothing happens ...'

He was looking deep into Mustapha's eyes now. His eyeballs were rolling constantly in fear. His knees were noiselessly moving against each other like two enemies, coming face to face and pulling apart.

Mustapha pulled his face away from the book and asked, 'So the job you said you'd agreed to ... was it ... this man ...' Before he could finish, the man glared at him. The question stayed incomplete.

Mustapha began to listen to the sound of the train. The man did not take his eyes off Mustapha. After some time, Mustapha opened the book. Sniffed. Turned the pages casually. Looked at the first chapter. Began to read.

'Read it aloud.'

Mustapha looked up.

'If you're reading, read it aloud,' the man said. 'I am tired. Need to sleep.'

Mustapha looked puzzled.

'The sight of a book makes me sleepy,' the man said. 'I will sleep quickly if I hear it.' He leaned back in his seat.

The sound of the train would drown out Mustapha's voice sometimes. He would read above it then. He read out eight or nine pages, then glanced at the man. He hadn't slept.

'Not sleeping?'

'I will. You keep reading.'

Running his finger on the page, Mustapha tried to find the line where he'd stopped. He found it and read aloud: 'They cut off the noses of all those who had breathed the scent of freedom.'

Mustapha walked home in the dark. When he reached the yard of the school, he wanted to pray. He pressed his head on the earth's great feet. In his prayer, the writer appeared. Umma came. The tipper-lorry driver Sura, he came too. The man came. So did Bappa, his sister and Chandran. And so, everyone, every single one, came. The night slumbered on like a baby.

Holiday Fun

It is only when people get together that stories are born. They are always half truth, half lies. The Decameron opens with a group of friends seeking refuge in storytelling from the fear of pestilence and death. Many of the stories thus born were obscene. So, too, is this story. Only that here, the friends soon abandoned storytelling to start a game.

They were like the refugees from the plague in *The Decameron*. Only, they were escaping the monotony of work, the four of them—Dharmapalan, Asokan, Vinayan and Das. They gathered in Room No. 70 of Nandavanam Lodge that Sunday, as usual, around a bottle of liquor. After the first peg, the room would turn into a confession-box echoing with hushed voices. Then, in the zigzagging and tumbling of voices, it would quickly transform into a washing machine. By the time they finished and left, the room would be filled with a stink and dirt worse than a filthy public toilet. Fated only to be reopened next

Sunday, the stench and litter would be imprisoned behind a big lock.

Perhaps that's why they decided to ditch the usual criticism of the government, the rant about bedroom squabbles, the description of the body of the young girl one brushed against in the street or on the bus, and instead, decided to either tell stories, or better still, play a game.

But they discovered the trouble with storytelling after a quick discussion. Be it a discussion, be it gossip, all would fit well into a story. In fact, you could even claim that your doctor's prescription was a story, provided you gave it a good title. But if you started a new story, then characters who became gods through the retelling could enter any time. Like Maricha, who had taken the form of a golden deer and lured Rama away in the Ramayana, these characters would beguile you with their smiles and subtle signals, and draw you further and further into the wild.

By the time you finally realised that you had been duped, it was too late. Then there would be just one way to exit the tale. Through a game. And so they abandoned the story and decided to play police-and-thief.

Those among the four who were struggling to recall that game from childhood were helped by Dharmapalan, who refreshed their memory. Four players, four pieces of paper. On these, write four names: King, Minister, Police, Thief—and then fold the chits. Each of them would then randomly choose one chit. The person who picked the chit with Police written on it had to guess who the Thief was. If he called the King 'Thief', he would be whipped five times. If he called the Minister 'Thief', he would receive three whiplashes. In the end, the Thief would be tried.

They had a drink before the game. Asokan wrote the names on pieces of paper, folded them twice, shook them inside his cupped palms, and threw them on the table. Each of them picked up a piece. Dharmapalan poured the second round of drinks.

Asokan said, 'I am the Police.'

'Good. After all, the journalist is a policeman of sorts,' teased Vinayan. 'The police feed shit and piss to prisoners, and journalists feed us with words that are way more disgusting.'

That upset Asokan. 'You better shut your trap, or else …'

Dharmapalan intervened. 'No quarrels today, please.'

Asokan and Vinayan fell silent. Asokan finished another peg.

Finding the thief is the policeman's job. Asokan looked at Dharmapalan. He was smoking, sending circles of smoke towards the ceiling. Vinayan was picking his teeth, mining something from his gums. Das was smiling, eyes fixed on Asokan's face. Who was the thief—the Road Transport officer Dharmapalan, Vinayan from the Registration Department, or Das, the tuition master? With the fire of two pegs in his belly, Asokan let his curious eyes wander in search of the thief in that semi-circle.

'If you are mistaken, you get whipped,' reminded Das. Asokan's zeal dimmed and his palms began to ache.

'Let's change the penalty,' he suggested. 'Two hundred rupees instead of five whiplashes; one hundred for three.'

The others nodded.

Asokan donned the policeman's keen gaze and re-entered the semi-circle. Dharmapalan was most likely the thief. His idols were the tyrannical minister C. P. Ramaswami Iyer and the oppressive and violent police officer Jayaram Padikkal, the man who went around with Prime Minister Indira Gandhi's photo in his pocket during the Emergency. A staunch devotee of Lord Rama. Sweet-talker. Religiously shared a part of the bribes he received with the gods. He joked that the penchant for illicit sexual excess was passed down generations among Brahmins, and justified his sexcapades thus. He must be the thief, Asokan decided. But he stood to lose two hundred rupees if he was wrong—good God! He downed another drink.

Dharmapalan and Vinayan had finished theirs too. They snacked on the peanuts and watched the alertness in Asokan's eyes.

'I am going to catch the thief,' he declared.

The others nodded in agreement.

'The thief among us is right here—Dharmapalan!'

Vinayan and Das turned to him. Dharmapalan was unfazed. He wiped his lips and asked in a voice that didn't sound like his, 'Who said that?'

Asokan looked into his reddened eyes and faltered a bit, but soon picked himself up and said, 'You are the thief, Dharma!'

Dharmapalan guffawed. His laughter echoed around the room like the flapping of the wings of a large bird, and soon subsided. The others were looking at him. He thrust his laugh quickly into the depths of his throat like he were slipping a dagger into its sheath, and held out his piece of paper—King.

Asokan looked away sheepishly.

'Two hundred,' said Dharmapalan.

Asokan put the money on the table.

'Okay, now catch the thief,' Dharmapalan raised his voice.

Asokan turned to Vinayan and Das. Vinayan smiled at him. Asokan sensed that the smile was sarcastic and was directed at him. Vinayan stopped smiling then, and taking a toothpick, got ready to retrieve the remnants of the peanuts from inside his cavities. Das kept drinking, unfurling the newspaper he held now and then and reading it in snatches, as though it were a curry to be tasted between sips.

Asokan looked at Vinayan. He had begun to scour his gums. *He* is the thief. Perpetually in contempt of the world. Arrogant, self-centred—I, I, forever. Lends out his entire salary on killer-interest rates, and lives a life of comfort at his wife's. Thinks nothing of the world whatsoever, thinks only about himself. Reinforces his friendship with Dharmapalan through an invisible sacred thread drawn out of periodic claims about his father and grandfather being Brahmins. Who else could be the thief?

'Hey, Policeman, who is the thief?' Dharmapalan's voice boomed.

'Dharma, give me some more time,' Asokan said.

'Not Dharma,' Dharmapalan corrected him haughtily. 'The King.'

'Forgive me, O King,' Asokan replied. 'I have caught the thief.'

Dharmapalan looked at each of them in turn, stretched his arms out and asked dramatically, 'Really, Policeman? Then tell me, who is he?'

His performance made Vinayan and Das smile at each other.

Asokan bowed to Dharmapalan and announced: 'O King! This bearded chap here, he is the thief!'

Dharmapalan shot a glance at Vinayan, who was sitting next to him and still searching for food lodged in his cavities. 'Hey, bearded fellow, are you the thief? My policeman thinks so.'

Vinayan put aside the toothpick, and took out the crumpled piece of paper from his pocket. He opened it and held it out to Dharmapalan.

Dharmapalan laughed out aloud. 'Hey, you policeman, do you know who this is?'

'No,' Asokan shook his head.

'This is my Minister!' He then demanded: 'A hundred rupees!'

Asokan, Dharmapalan and Vinayan now turned towards Das, who sat with his head bent, looking rather sozzled after his third drink.

'O King,' said Asokan, pointing at Das, 'this man's the thief.'

'This one?' asked Dharmapalan. 'What did he steal?'

'I am not a thief,' said Das, tipsily.

The others laughed.

'Policeman, what is his name?' asked Dharmapalan. 'What are the charges against him?'

Asokan gulped down another peg and said, 'O King, I saw him inside your inner chambers. I overpowered him after a scuffle. Then I tied up his limbs and bound him to a tree. But even after hours of questioning, he did not reveal his name or native place. But he kept boasting that he would loot the palace and give away all the gold and grains amassed here to the poor, and that he would exile all the bribe-taking and philandering ministers. He also said that the people hate this reign and that the lower castes would rule this land, and he even asked me to give up the slavish work of a policeman and join him!'

No sooner had he finished than Dharmapalan jumped up from his chair and kicked Das hard on his face. Das fell flat on his back.

To Vinayan, who leapt up and held his hand saying 'Dharma, what the hell are you doing,' he said, 'Vinaya, you are a minister. You should know that it is my duty

as King to punish those who talk waywardly like this.'
Vinayan bowed his head.

Planting another kick on Das, who was trying to get
up, Dharmapalan said, 'You thief! You dared to say that
you'll plunder my palace? That you'll exile us?'

Das lay on the floor. He looked up at Dharmapalan.
His mind was standing on the shaky stilts of three pegs.
The sight of Dharmapalan with his leg upraised like a
character in the *Chavittunatakam* play made him laugh. 'I
am a tuition master. My job is to give lessons to children.'

Dharmapalan flew into a rage. 'Minister, why is this
fellow babbling?'

'O King, he is intoxicated. That's why,' said Asokan.

Vinayan and Asokan lifted Das up from the floor and
made him stand against the wall.

'I order that this enemy of the nation be hanged to
death!' Dharmapalan roared.

Asokan and Vinayan bowed low and stood aside. Das
propped up his wobbling body against the wall.

'It is time,' said Dharmapalan, turning to Vinayan and
Asokan, 'to hang this enemy of the nation. Is everything
ready?'

They nodded affirmatively.

Asokan pulled off the jute thread from the food
packets, made a noose, and put it around Das's neck.

'Chhi, what a farce!' said Dharmapalan, loosening it.
'Isn't a stronger rope available?'

They searched the whole room and returned, disappointed. 'No, Your Highness, this is all that we have.'

Dharmapalan looked at Das. His hand tightened around the liquor bottle. He swung it hard; it hit the table and shattered with a loud noise. Then he sprang towards Das with great speed. Das slid down, collapsing, eyes nearly popping out, the bottle stuck deep in his guts.

And so the game of police-and-thief wound up. Room No. 70 in the Nandavanam Lodge was locked once more, until the next holiday.

Beyond the Canal, Beyond the Yard

No sooner had Kurudi Ummachi—Granny-No-see—got back home from Africa than she climbed into bed, complaining of exhaustion. Zulfat went to the kitchen to make the batter for the next day's dosa. After some time, Granny called out to her, asking for some water. When she went into the bedroom with a glass full of water, Granny was lying on her stomach.

'Hey, Granny, what's this? Lying down all day? Get up!' said Zulfat.

Granny-No-see sat up and sighed. 'Been verr...y tired after we returned from Africa.'

'I feel okay,' said Zulfat.

Sipping the water, Granny asked her, 'Did you touch that zebra?'

'Yes, of course I did. What about you?'

'It ran away when I went up close. So I just went ahead and touched the lion.'

'That's a huge fib! You wouldn't have touched the lion—I'd have seen!' teased Zulfat.

'You think I let you see everything I do?' Granny-No-see sounded displeased.

'Alright, so from now on, you can go all by yourself—to America, Russia, wherever!' Zulfat got up to take the glass and strode off to the kitchen.

Afterwards, Granny sat on the cot for some time. Then she got up too, and went to the kitchen. Zulfat was busy grinding soaked pulses to a batter.

'Don't get so easily pissed off,' Granny told her. 'Without you, how's this blind woman to travel around the world?' She caressed Zulfat's curls fondly.

'So then be good!' Zulfat said, wiping her hand on the edge of the grinding stone. 'If you get too big for your boots, I won't come with you ever.'

Granny fell silent. A magpie hopped in the garden. A spider heaved itself upside-down on to the wooden ceiling of their house.

'Go to bed please. I'll be there in a moment,' said Zulfat, pushing back the curls that had fallen on her forehead.

Granny turned to leave. It was then that Zulfat noticed that the papaya tree outside had fallen.

'Ayyo, our papaya tree has fallen down!'

'Good god!' Granny turned her head in the direction of the garden as if she could see the fallen tree. 'When did it happen? It was all right when we left for Africa, wasn't it?'

'Yes,' said Zulfat, looking at the tree again. 'I plucked two papayas just the other day.'

'Maybe there was a bad storm when we were away in Africa ...'

'That's possible,' agreed Zulfat.

Two squirrels were scampering around on the tree; a crow was pecking at a ripe fruit. Poor thing, thought Zulfat, looking at the fallen tree.

The bitter-gourd vines on the other side of the papaya tree looked ravaged. Someone had dug up all the tapioca and taken it away. It had to be the handiwork of Buffalo-Pillachan—he must have been drinking. It would make Granny furious, Zulfat knew. So she didn't say anything.

'What are you thinking?' Granny asked her.

'Oh, nothing,' she lied.

'It was such a bountiful tree,' Granny murmured, and then she got up and went to her room.

When Zulfat had finished making the curry for dinner, she went inside and found Granny standing by the window, looking out as if she were gazing at something intently.

'What are you looking at?' Zulfat asked.

'Come here, my girl,' Granny called.

Zulfat went and stood behind her.

'See?' Granny said. 'The sun is setting into the sea!'

Zulfat could see the sun above Kuttassar's house, beyond Granny's shoulder. It looked at them indifferently as it sank quickly behind the leaves of a mango tree.

'Will anyone believe that you can see Kanyakumari from here?' Granny asked. 'It's Allah's secret boon! Make sure you don't tell anyone about it!'

'My dear Granny', Zulfat said, gently shepherding her towards the cot, 'I won't tell a soul. Just make sure you don't tell anyone either.'

Granny did not like Zulfat's reply.

'Did you cut up the fallen tree and put it under the coconut tree?'

'No, I will do it tomorrow.'

'This is the trouble. Tomorrow, tomorrow, tomorrow. Put off, put off, put off everything! Why can't you finish it up quick? Tell me if you can't—I will do it!'

Zulfat changed the topic.

'Wasn't right, really, not fair at all—you were watching the sunset alone.'

'My child, I was taking a nap when the three seas called out to me. They were right here, just outside the window, calling—hey, take a look, we are here!'

Zulfat thought she saw two suns rise from Granny's eyes which were covered with the milky foam of sea waves.

The other day, their neighbour Sumathy, who had returned from a trip to Kanyakumari had described the sights there to Granny. When she left, Granny had said, 'Such good luck! Her husband lets her go only to temples, but she can go to so many places on that pretext!'

'My darling Granny', Zulfat had consoled her, 'we have gone to so many places—Japan, China …Has Sumathy travelled anywhere around there?'

Zulfat lay the table for dinner.

Granny found two tiny stones in the gruel, and it irritated her.

'You didn't clean the rice carefully!'

'I did,' said Zulfat, feeling for stones in her own bowl.

'I had told you, I'll do it if you can't.'

'I am sorry—please let it go,' Zulfat pleaded, serving Granny another spoonful of the chammandi.

After dinner, Zulfat cleared up, latched the door and went into the bedroom. Granny-No-see was sitting cross-legged.

'No plans to sleep tonight?' Zulfat asked.

'See if we have any more of that Kaattumaakan's books? Could you read out loud to me?'

'Not Kaattumaakan, how many times do I have to tell you?' Zulfat snapped. 'It is S. K. Pottekkatt, the travel writer.'

'I can say his name only that way. Why couldn't they have given him a better name? Anyway, com' on, you read!'

Zulfat took out *Nile Diary*. Granny-No-See leaned back against the wall. Zulfat sat on the edge of the cot and began to read aloud. 'The Nile becomes the Murchison Waterfall when it meets the rock formations between Kyoga and Albert. Here we see the 200-feet-broad river turn into a 25-foot sheet of water, and hurtle down the gap between the rocks.'

'Koché, how about we visit this waterfall tomorrow?'

'I have to go to class. Let's make it next Saturday.'

Granny-No-see hmmed to that and said she was going to bed. Zulfat switched the lights off and went to sleep hugging her. But Granny got up in the middle of the night, found her way around to the windows and doors, and made sure they were bolted. When she heard something move outside, she held Zulfat close.

Her real name was Rabia. She was sightless at birth. People had called her No-see ever since she was a child. When she grew old, they began to accord her some respect and called her Granny-No-see. Zulfat was her daughter's child.

Her husband Kunhali was the only man around these places who had seen the world. It was in the middle of his travels that Rabia's father had brought him home one day. He had a bad leg and so couldn't go anywhere beyond the local market. It was not easy in those days to find someone like Kunhali who could tell you about the world. Kunhali had travelled to Kaippuzha, Koothattukulam, Poonjar, Peerumedu, Kavanattinkara, Mohamma, and many other places. Besides, he was going to work in a press that was soon to be set up in Kottayam. He had been trained at the Ravi Varma Press in Bombay, at Donavali. He had travelled on a train many times.

Rabia's father had allowed him to stay in a small extension of their house. Every evening, Kunhali would tell tales from his travels to the locals gathered in the frontyard. It was quite peculiar. When the India-China war was going on, he managed to scare people stiff. He would draw one line and name it China. Next to it, he would draw another and call it India. And then he would draw two more and call them America and Russia. In his map, these four countries were adjacent to each other. And were long straight lines, of course. *If anyone touches India, Russia will drop a bomb. If anyone touches China, America will drop a bomb.* In between, he would draw some more lines, each a nation. Granny-No-see's frontyard could go to bed many a day only after it was marked all over with such lines. Seeing them, No-see's mother would say: Oh, under all those jackfruit and mango leaves, a big striped tiger! No matter how thoroughly she swept the lines away each morning, it would still stride out of Kunhali's leg at nightfall—as many, many places, many, many tales. No-see and her mother would hear them all from inside the house, through a window opened just a little.

No-see was not allowed to go outside the house because she was blind. She had visited her mother's family home once or twice. On the way there, she would keep asking about the sounds she heard and about the roads they crossed. Soon her father had stopped even those trips because her questions irritated him.

He would mention Kunhali now and then. Lucky fellow, how many places he's visited! She agreed. She was delighted when she came to know that he had decided to marry her off to Kunhali. The neighbours told her, now you can go to so many places with your man. Even if you can't see, he's going to tell you all about it really nicely. And you can walk all around!

No-see was also eager to know about all the places Kunhali had already been to. She told Zulfat much later that she had agreed to the marriage, though Kunhali was much older than her, only to hear about his travels. But after he married her, Kunhali did not tell a single story; neither did he take her anywhere. He would, however, go on his jaunts sometimes. When people came over to find out what he had said to her about his trips, No-see would tell them that she was under strict instructions not to reveal anything. That would make them quite envious of her. When they left, she would weep.

In the middle of all this, she gave birth to three children. The first two were stillborn. The third was Zulfat's mother Sahiya.

One day, No-see's man was sitting in Kesavan Nair's teashop in the market, when a Muslim chap from Kannur turned up. He was asking if there was a shop available for rent. When they asked him what he needed it for, he said that he just wanted to meditate over there. They asked why he needed a shop to meditate and whether it wasn't enough to go meditate in the forest, and he told them that he had met a fakir in Kashmir who meditated in a shop, and that he had told him to do the same. Kunhali instantly wanted to hear about his travels. Gradually, it became clear that there was no place the man hadn't visited. Kunhali grew fond of him.

He hadn't married off his daughter yet, expecting her to find a good bridegroom someday. Now, in her forty-fifth year, he married Sahiya off to this old man from Kannur.

When she became pregnant five months after the wedding, the old man left her, claiming that it wasn't his child. Two days later, Kunhali left No-see, saying, the loss of face was too much for him to bear. No-see tried to console her daughter. She tried to tell her not to bother, but it was futile. The third day after she gave birth to Zulfat, Sahiya threw herself on the railway tracks.

No-see raised Zulfat right in front of the people who had sighed and exclaimed about how a blind woman would ever raise a child, that too, a girl. When she was old enough to walk, Zulfat gripped No-see's hand, and No-see gripped hers, and together they walked out of the house.

Once Zulfat brought back a book called *London Yatra* from the library. No-see began to laugh at the title. Why are you laughing, asked Zulfat, and she said, 'My father once told me, a long time back, "To go to the toilet, you say, I am going to London!"' Maybe this is a tale about crapping, Zulfat thought. But when she read it, she found that it was indeed about travelling to London. She read it out, and No-see listened to the whole book. And then, she decided she wanted to make a trip there. That's how

Granny-No-see and Zulfat, who had never even gone past the road-junction, managed to go to London.

They got on the bus from the Ambady junction and got off at Chungam. When they stopped at the Varissery junction, Zulfat whispered in No-see's ear, the next stop is London. No-see nodded gravely. Zulfat stood on the Chungam bridge and looked down; the Meenachil was flowing quietly, as usual. How's the current in the Thames, asked Granny-No-see. Thinking how sharp her memory was, Zulfat said, oh, very strong. There was a small canoe approaching. There's a big boat approaching the bridge, Zulfat announced. Standing on the Waterloo Bridge, the two of them looked around. You know what, someone's cleaning the spire of St Paul's Cathedral, Zulfat said. Where, I can't see, replied Granny-No-see, and Zulfat pointed it out to her. Yes, what fun it must be, Granny said, brimming with happiness. Shall we go to Russell Park before we leave, Zulfat asked. Yes, of course, said Granny-No-see. It would be a shame not to see it after we've come all this way!

After some time, seeing someone coming towards them, Zulfat leaned towards Granny and whispered, I think that's T.S. Eliot. Let me see, Granny said, and took a look. Oh yes, that's him. Krishnan, who wrote verse, had just walked past them. Zulfat said, ooh, how keen! That was him indeed!' Granny-No-see smiled smugly. Maybe he's off to write a poem. Notice how puffed-up he looks.

It was after the London tour that Zulfat and Granny began to travel regularly. Kuttampuram became Venice; Athirampuzha, the Vatican; Kumarakom, Russia; and the wall behind Thekkedathu Mana's property, the Great Wall of China! The local folks had no clue where the two kept going off to. Sometimes, when the neighbours asked, Granny would say, Zulfat needed a sacred amulet and they were off to see the Musaliar to get one. To others, she would say, Zulfat still peed in bed, and so needed a holy thread on her arm. Zulfat warned her sternly to give up that story, and so Granny had to stop dishing it out.

That morning, when they went to Maniyaparambu, Granny predicted that the trip to Africa would be a bit rough. To get to Maniyaparambu, they had to cut across the Raviswaram fields and walk through the yards of some households there. How dense these forests are, Granny, said Zulfat. Can barely see a thing. Gripping her hand firmly, Granny said, oh be careful, there may be elephants! Before she had uttered the words, an elephant appeared before them. Here, Granny, whispered Zulfat. A bull elephant? Granny whispered back. Yes, indeed, said Zulfat. That was Madhavi Kaniyatti's varikka jackfruit tree. Standing under its trunk that bulged out like an elephant's forehead, Granny touched Zulfat involuntarily. When they had walked ahead some distance, Granny grabbed her arm and stopped her. Look here, she said, do you see the wild bison? Zulfat peered through the leaves. You saw? Granny asked. No, said Zulfat. It ran off before I looked. Be careful. Not a sound. We should listen for every little rustle. No use walking around with just the eyes wide open. I may not be with you always, reminded Granny.

They walked past a tall konna tree, and Zulfat said, ah, here's a giraffe! Granny's foot brushed against a small bush, and she said, there's the wild rabbit. And then they brushed against the nettles; it stung and they said, oh so many leeches! And so they walked and walked, and saw all sorts of forests in Africa.

When Zulfat went to her classes, Granny-No-see had nothing to do. She would just lounge on the veranda. Some people passing by would stop for a chat. That's how she came to know about the jaggery-boss going on Hajj, from Mariumma.

Mariumma was from the southern part of the village, a woman who was forever walking in and out of houses, talking, talking, talking, all day long. Her children were all in the Gulf. She had told Granny-No-see well in advance that she should not believe the local shrews who spread the rumour that she was in the habit of borrowing her daughter-in-law's gold jewellery.

'That Mammath has gone off on Hajj. Of course he can—doesn't he have tonnes of money?' Mariumma made it sound like a complaint.

'But why're you thrusting a lit piece of firewood under that statement?' asked Granny-No-see. 'Let him go.'

'Who said he shouldn't?' said Mariumma, putting a piece of betelnut into her mouth. 'I am only pissed off seeing that he's going even after doing god-awful things.'

'If he's done god-awful things, then he'll pay.' Granny-No-see spread lime on a betel-leaf.

'Does God punish like that?' Mariumma sounded doubtful. 'If he falls to his knees and weeps in Mecca, begging forgiveness, God may forgive him ... Then what ...?'

'Yes, then what can one do? Nothing! Why upset yourself over that?'

'Yes,' admitted Mariumma, spitting long into the yard. 'Why indeed should I bother?'

'Anyhow, he's a fortunate fellow. He's going to Mecca. What luck!' Granny leaned back on a pillar in the veranda.

'Hey No-see, even if God gave you luck, what good would it be? You can see nothing, and you have a girl at home that you can't leave alone. But look at me. I lack nothing. I have money, health, but still, where's the luck? Maybe God doesn't want to see you and me.'

Because she suspected that Mariumma would start ranting at God next, Granny-No-see got up and said, 'It's almost time—the girl will be back, hungry like hell.

If I don't have something ready for her to eat, she will go crazy. Let me go make some ada or kozhikkatta.'

Mariumma too stood up saying, 'Okay, I will leave now.'

When Zulfat was drinking her tea, Granny told her about Kizhakketil Mammath going on Hajj. Zulfat finished her tea and ada, and went off to wash her clothes in the canal.

At night, when they were about to go to bed, Mammath's Hajj came up again. 'Even if one can't go on Hajj, wouldn't it be wonderful to go on a visit to Mecca?' said Granny, almost to herself. Zulfat had fallen asleep rather quickly. When she woke sometime in the middle of the night, Granny was sitting up on the cot.

'Not sleeping, Granny?' she asked.

'Yes,' Granny said, but continued to sit there.

'Granny ...' Zulfat called out.

Granny did not reply.

'You want to go to Mecca, right?'

She nodded.

Zulfat took Granny to the Vattakkotta the next day.

Seeing them walk past Alummoottil, Mannan Gopi asked Sivaraman, who was making beedis sitting inside Aniyan Pillai's teashop, 'Hey, where do the old woman and kid keep going off to now and again? They go pretty often.'

'Let them go wherever they like,' said Sivaraman, continuing his work. 'What's it to you?'

'Ah, that won't do,' said Mannan Gopi, scratching his leg with his machete. 'What if they're up to some hanky-panky?'

'That's true,' said the barber Majid. 'I've seen the two hanging around in many places.'

'My dear Majid, the other day, I was at Maniyaparambu, and had just gulped down two pegs, when these two came and stood there, laughing and talking goodness knows what all. I thought I was drunk, but the boatman Vasu also said the same! Something's wrong.'

'Yes, yes, something is wrong. Look at the girl. All grown up, looking like a luscious green gourd. That is what's wrong!' Majid said. 'If things continue the way they are, some eagle will swoop down, grab her, and fly away.'

Granny-No-see gripped Zulfat's hand harder than usual.

'What is it, Granny?' she asked. 'My arm aches.'

Granny did not loosen her hold.

As they climbed up the path to Vattakotta, parting the wild bushes, Zulfat exclaimed, 'What a crowd!'

Granny did not reply.

'Oh, so you're all puffed-up about going to Mecca, are you?' she teased.

Granny still held her arm firmly, and kept mum. That was rather unusual for her. It made Zulfat wary, and so she became silent too.

When they reached the foot of the Vattakkotta rock, Zulfat said, 'Granny, from here you can go to Mecca by yourself.'

Granny eased her grip and kissed Zulfat's forehead. Zulfat stood below, watching her climb each step with utmost care.

Granny heard the prayers of Mecca rise in the air. She could feel their righteous touch in the wind.

She circumambulated the Kaaba seven times and prayed.

Zulfat stood carving their names on a rockface with her nails. In between, a bird flew up, sat on the branch of a tree, chattered something, and then flew away.

Seeing Granny come down the steps as though she were holding someone's hand, Zulfat could not but marvel.

When they were walking back home, she asked, 'What did you pray for at the Kaaba?'

'That's a secret,' Granny said, hugging her close. 'Kids don't have to know.'

When they got into bed that night, Zulfat said, 'When you came down the steps today, it was as if someone was holding your hand. How quickly you came down! I was worried how you would come down by yourself ...'

Granny smiled and told Zulfat, 'Go to sleep now.'

They woke up only when Nani Amma came with the milk.

'What sort of sleeping is this?' she asked.

Granny took the milk from her.

'Saw the two of you take off to Vattakkotta yesterday. Where were you going?' Nani Amma asked.

Granny-No-see went close to her and whispered, 'I was going to Mecca.'

'What!' Nani Amma could not believe it.

'Yes, you heard right. I just visited Mecca.'

Nani Amma stood there for a few minutes, puzzled. Then she quickly walked over to the northern side of the house where Zulfat was taking out charcoal powder to brush her teeth with, and told her: 'Koché, I think your grandmother has lost her marbles.'

'Why, what happened?'

'When I asked where you had gone yesterday, she said she'd gone to Mecca!'

Zulfat was amused.

'What's going to happen to this girl if the old woman goes crazy, oh god!' Nani Amma sounded like she was asking herself. Then she quickly went away.

Zulfat went to the kitchen where Granny was making coffee.

'So you told her about the Mecca trip—when you're always saying, tell no one any secrets?'

She sat down near the hearth, and asked, 'In that case, tell me the secret you told God ...?'

Granny-No-see took her hand. When her fingers closed around her wrist, it hurt a little, but Zulfat did not complain. Granny pulled her close. They did not speak. Zulfat leaned into her; she could hear the prayer inside her chest. Then she held her arms and asked, 'Shouldn't we go and see Kaattumaakan's waterfall?'

Granny-No-see laughed.

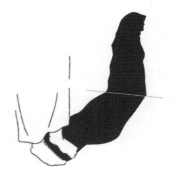

Calling to Prayer

Loomed he close, with dark intent,
o'er the Prophet's hallowed head,
that in deep prayer did often bend,
and bend it did with love blessed,
And often did He beg the Lord,
'Forgive Thy people when they err'.

And then there bloomed a tiny word,
'Allah!'—
Such was the piety it stirred,
so fine, so smooth, so full of love,
the sword that sought the Master's Head,
slipp'd off the hand that loomed above.

'Allah', Vallathol Narayana Menon

'I want to kiss our HOD's hairy wrist,' said Deepa.

'I want to tell John from the English Department that I like him,' said Jyothi.

'I want to watch a movie with Ashraf', said Shameena.

Raziya alone was silent.

'You have nothing to say?' asked Jyothi.

Nothing, Raziya shook her head.

'Look, don't be such a killjoy. We've just one more month of classes. Before that, we must do at least one thing we really, really want to.' Deepa sounded miffed.

Raziya was unaffected; she continued to look out the window.

'My dear Raziya, please open your mouth.' Shameena held her face with both hands and turned her towards them. 'None of this may happen after we're all married and packed off. That's why … tell us if you have something in mind.'

Raziya pulled her veil over her head and looked at them, smiling slightly. Her friends looked at her eagerly.

'I have something I want to do. But will it be possible?'

'Dearie, do you want to hug the principal? Or do you want to down a peg or two? Or sleep with someone?' Shameena asked her. 'Tell us what it is—be bold! We're here for you, your friends!'

Raziya was silent for a few moments, and then, with her usual smile, she said, 'I want to call the azaan … the prayer.'

Silence pushed its way into their midst. Shameena pushed it back out vehemently, and equally quickly. 'Are you crazy? Make sure no one else hears this!'

Raziya continued to smile and asked, 'But didn't you just say you're going to stand by me no matter what it is …?'

'Yes, yes, we're all with you,' Shameena said, sounding a little fearful now. 'But we can't support these sorts of things.'

'Is it that much trouble?' Jyothi was curious.

'Yes, faith and God … touch those two and everything will burn! Dear Raziya, tell us if there's anything else you want to do.'

Raziya did not respond.

'Think again, and find something exciting.' Shameena put her arm around Raziya. 'We don't have to decide right now.'

When they were returning from college, Jyothi asked, 'Do you really want to call the azaan so badly?'

Raziya nodded affirmatively.

She had gone to Thiruvananthapuram with her parents when she was five. Seeing an animal inside a cage in the zoo for the very first time, she had begun to weep. It won't hurt you, her parents had assured her, but still she had wept. Open the door and let it go, she had sobbed, and her father had said, no, no, it will hurt us. Raziya had kept weeping, refusing to listen to him. They had had to leave. Her father was angry; never will I take this pest anywhere again, he had vowed. That was a Friday. Her father went to the Palayam mosque for the Juma prayer. Raziya and her mother waited for him in the veranda of a closed shop in the Connemara Market opposite the mosque. She was still sobbing when the call to azaan from the mosque reached her side. Raziya looked at it and marvelled at its sweetness. She watched it bloom far above the sunlight in the noon sky. She stopped crying and fell asleep. By the time they returned to Kottayam, the music of the azaan was dangling on her earlobes invisibly like an ornament.

She returned home from college and was just about stepping into the house when her mother called out, 'Hey, did you hear? Ashraf Mama's son said he likes you a lot.'

Umma was like that. Whatever she needed to say, she would spit out. Not a care about who might hear, where she was—no way.

Raziya turned sharply to check if any of their neighbours had heard. Then she asked, '*Ethu*? Which one? The fair-skinned, muscular one …? … And what did *you* say?'

'I told Ashraf Mama that you are going to join coaching classes for the IAS entrance exam after your college, and that we aren't keen at this point. Then he said, we can send her there after the wedding. I said no.'

Raziya laughed. 'That's just great. Let's not tell Vappa!'

After dinner, when they were chatting, Raziya told Umma, 'You know, today Deepa, Shameena and the others were asking me, what's your one big desire?'

'And what did you say?'

'I told them.'

'I am asking you what that is, the one big desire ...'

Raziya moved closer to Umma and whispered in her ear. Umma giggled, saying she was ticklish.

'Ooh, so you are a nubile wench, are you, to feel all ticklish?'

'Why, what's wrong with that?' Umma struck back. 'I was married off at fourteen. Otherwise, I too would have been prancing around all by myself just like you!'

'Oh Umma, people will start asking if you're my younger sister. Will that make you happy?'

'Why did you sneak in the question about what makes me happy? Isn't it true? Yes, it's been a grind—you chewed on my breasts till you were three and a half, and it's been a hard task to keep them standing firm since then!'

'That's the power of the Balaswagandhaadi oil and then you and Vappa ...'

'Saying wicked things, uh?'

The house filled with their laughter.

'Now tell me.'

'Okay,' said Raziya, looking around warily. 'I want to call the azaan.'

Umma stared at her for a moment, not sure what to say. Then she got up and went away. If Umma didn't like something, she would never say no or don't do it. Her response would be silence.

That night, she did not speak to Raziya. When everyone fell asleep, Raziya asked her Maker: 'Am I wrong to want this?'

The cloud that had masked the moon slid away. A sliver of light entered her room.

When they were sitting around and chatting the next day after lunch, Deepa ran in and grabbed Shameena's shoulders, announcing triumphantly, 'I kissed!'

Nobody believed her at first. Deepa brought her lips close to Shameena's face and asked, 'See, can't you see the steam rising?'

Shameena said, 'Yes, a Manipravala scent.'

Deepa described with great literary flourish how she had got a copy of the *Kerala Panineeyam* from Varma Sir, who was standing between the bookshelves in the library, and how she had dived like a kingfisher and snatched some drops of sweat from his hairy wrist. Before she finished, they were all glued to the library windows.

'Dumbstruck!' Jyothi exclaimed.

'Since you touched his *paani*, you are from this day, Panini!' Raziya told Deepa.

'I am going to tell John from the Department of English that I like him,' Jyothi said and went off.

She was panting lightly as she approached him. That's probably why he kind of measured her up and let her know that he was in love with his classmate Krishnakumar.

Jyothi was a bit taken aback, but then she collected herself and replied, 'Okay, that's fine, but I still like you.'

John looked like he was going to cry. 'No, Jyothi,' he pleaded, 'please think of me as your brother ...'

Her impatience got the better of that plea. 'That won't work. I am tripping over brother after brother at home!'

John looked at her helplessly. Jyothi pretended her failure was no big deal, and almost chewed up her lips that threatened to break into a sob. She turned around and walked a few steps, and then, even her feet did not know where she was running away to in such hurry.

For a few days, a light sadness hung about her like a mild breeze. She came out of it when she went to the movies with Shameena. Shameena was sitting with Ashraf. Ashraf's friend sat next to her. When the lights went down in the theatre, the friend asked her, 'It's awfully cold in here. Can I please hug you for a bit?'

In that tiny pause before she could summon up words like 'you asshole', 'bastard' and so on, a soft, warm arm wrapped itself around Jyothi's shoulders. Before the lights came on during the interval, it slipped off gently. This did not lead to a kiss; nor did the fingers wander anywhere else. When the movie was over, Ashraf's friend gave her a beaming smile.

'Oh, my clothes are in a mess,' Shameena said coyly when they were returning. 'Will people suspect?'

Jyothi didn't respond to that. Instead, she said, 'Maybe that boy was really feeling cold...'

Time flew, and the calendar kept reminding the girls of its swift pace. Raziya's friends were sad that nothing seemed to be working for her. There was just one more week before the college closed.

'Hey Raziya,' said Jyothi, 'let go of that wish. Find something new, please ...?'

'Yes, any other naughty whim, and we are with you.' Shameena touched her own head and said, 'God promise!'

Raziya was quiet for some time, and then she said, 'This is my only wish.'

'This girl's daft,' said Deepa, angrily. 'We're just fooling about, and she gets all serious. Let's stop this here.'

'Yes, that's better,' Shameena agreed. 'There's a limit to everything. No need to cross it and cause a revolution!'

'Shamee,' said Raziya, 'I didn't say we should start a revolution. I just told you my wish. That's the one wish I've had since I was a kid.'

'Surely, at our age, you'd want something different. Why don't you pick a wish like that? Why insist on impossible things?'

'Why're you getting so mad at her for that?' Jyothi asked Deepa.

'Actually, I am done,' said Deepa, picking up her bag and getting ready to leave. 'Shamee, I'm leaving; are you coming?'

As Shameena got ready to leave with Deepa, she gave Raziya a bit of advice: 'Girl, try to be a true believer.'

Jyothi could not tell what that meant. As they were walking towards the bus-stand, she asked Raziya, 'Do you really want to do it so badly?'

Raziya nodded.

'You want to call the azaan tomorrow?'

'No.'

'Which day then?'

'Next Friday, at the Juma prayer.'

Jyothi didn't know what the Juma prayer was, but she knew that Friday was the day.

'Let's go together, then,' said Jyothi.

'Where?'

'There's a wild place some ten-fifteen kilometres from here. There's no one there. Would that be okay with you?'

'Why not!' said Raziya, joyfully taking Jyothi's hand.

When she went to bed on Thursday night, Raziya recalled the sweetness of the call to prayer at the Palayam mosque, which she had heard at the age of five and savoured all the way back home. She had never again heard anything so sweet. She had later heard a powerful, magnetic call, one that drew her inner world towards it in the clock

Vappa had brought from the Gulf. In those moments, she thought that that music was an invitation to enter God's presence.

The next day, she stood in front of the college with her grandmother's prayer mat and some water in a large, covered water-jug. Jyothi soon joined her. She had brought along a boy, the same age as them.

'This is Ashraf's friend,' Jyothi said with a smile. 'Remember, I told you …?'

Raziya nodded.

'There's no bus to that place, and autos won't go either… You can go with him.'

Raziya was silent.

'Are you scared?' Jyothi asked.

Raziya just smiled, and then sat behind the boy on the bike.

They walked under tree branches that grew right into the darkness. The scent that wafted up from snake-skins left behind on the grassy path by newly-moulted snakes was totally new to Raziya. The creepers that hung from tree-branches trying to kiss the ground touched their necks like long fingers in the wind. Some of the branches brushed against their eyes.

'There's a wasps' nest,' the boy said, pointing towards a tree.

'I have never seen a wasps' nest before,' she said.

'Don't look if they come after you,' he laughed. 'Run for your life!'

Two young men had gone to the arrack-shop seeing a motorbike parked just outside the wild. Not finding anyone there, they had gone into the thickets. As they were walking, pushing aside the leaves and branches, they heard a male voice and then a female's. Their steps quickened. When they turned near a big tree, they saw Raziya and the boy.

'Young girl,' one said.

'The guy's pretty young as well,' said the other.

'Shouldn't we call the others too?' the first man asked, nodding.

'Yes, let's not waste time.'

They quickly made their way out.

One of the trees shed its leaves quickly, as if it were uttering many words at once.

Raziya asked the boy what the time was. He told her.

'This is west, right?' she asked to confirm.

'Yes.'

The two men came up along the road with two others. They trampled on the leaves and cut through the foliage with their machetes. Suddenly the air and the leaves and their feet were pushed into silence as the call rose in a woman's voice: Allah-u-Akbar. The music that had been mellowed by the touch of centuries soared up through the dark forest into the sky, and then dived into the roots that had lengthened into the depths of the soil.

When they came back, Raziya did not feel that the men on the road were strangers. She smiled at them. They did not smile back.

She went back to college with the boy, and they, to the arrack-seller's place.

Playing Dad

My father began to behave like a little kid, all of a sudden.
After he retired from the army, he began to spend most
of his time by himself inside his room. I would often see
through the gap in the window his menacing moustache,
reddish eyes, and his huge body sometimes moving among
the many things in that room, and staying completely still
and lifeless at other times.

I believed that all the people who stayed by themselves
were locked in some intense combat with God. He
would one day emerge triumphant from that room into
the world of ordinary folk with a smashing discovery, I
thought. I once even told Mother an absurd story about
how he'd someday enter into a contract with God that
would make the wheels run to one side, and vehicles, to
the other. Mother stooped even more with the weight
of that news. But now, here he is, running around the
house like a small child! In between, he hides behind the
pillars and peeps out. Goes around jumping joyfully at the
discovery of a long-lost coin from the darkness under his

cot. As we watch, Father's upright figure, his moustache and large bulging eyes look more and more unsightly.

Father has never spoken to me, not even once. He was distant from words themselves. The communication between us was made possible by grunts and gestures. I kept expecting that at least his index finger would give way to a basic 'ah' or that the call 'hey son' would replace the arching of his brows. But each time, his look would flash by like lightning, shaking me from the inside. For him, the glance was a weapon. I would often hide in a corner and watch him glance at Mother. Sometimes he would go stand in the veranda while some of the neighbour's hens foraged in our yard. He would just be looking at them, and they would run away, unable to bear the pain they felt. I wondered if the red in his eyes was from the life-force of people dissolved in it. And when one day he disappeared into one of the inner rooms, he left his gaze behind, perpetually awake, fixed on us forever. And now, here he stands, hiding behind the pillar, peeping out now and then, and saying, 'I want to go see the train!'

I went outside the house with him just once. That's when I saw the train for the first time. He did not tell me then that this was the train—the massive sound that shook my feet as it went by like a reptile tautened with unyielding muscles of iron. When that celebration of arrogance and power, hurtling on the rails carved by the sun had passed, I simply shut my eyes tight.

When we walked towards the paddy fields which the railway tracks cut through, he walked ahead of me, making sure he was always leading. He kicked the empty tin lying there as if it were a ball. It bounced on the uneven surface of the gravel, making an ugly sound, and disappeared into the thickets. Father went after it. He moved aside each leaf carefully and kicked it back into the gravel. Passers-by looked at him curiously. From the shops and the houses, eyes followed him. His body did not absorb the scorn that flowed from them. So they attacked me. I caught up with him and said, people are looking.

When we waited beside the fields through which the railway tracks passed, I looked at him. His gaze was fixed on the bend in the distance, from where an incoming train was visible. Some women who had gone to cut grass stood on the tracks and called out to him asking something. Their faces were hidden by sheaves of grass. He did not respond. He revolved around another world.

The train chugged up slowly from the bend in the field. Father waved his arms and jumped up and down. The engine driver must have found old man's prancing rather obscene. That was quite evident in his eyes, half hidden under his red turban, and on his grimacing lips. Many of the passengers looked at Father with wonder. Father waved to each of them. Not one of them even smiled back. Standing in the warmth generated by the wheels of the train upon the tracks once it had passed us by, Father waved again and again, expressing his joy at its lengthy journey. The intersecting lines drawn at the back of the train left behind a riddle: What were they? A multiplication sign or the marking of an error?

Each day we found something gone missing in the house. Some of those things were recovered from the attic or bathroom or the yard. Some were lost forever. Father hid some things. Threw away other things. Broke yet others.

I did not take it too seriously at first. But when it looked like Father's antics were going to empty out the house, I told Mother that it was getting too much. Mother didn't like my saying it.

One day I saw him standing by the well and peering inside. I was frightened. I went up behind him and looked into the well. Under the overgrowth on the rings of the wall, in a small pool of water, I saw our faces near each other's. Suddenly, he threw something inside. There was a resounding thud that climbed up to the surface, and the web of water broke and scattered, obscuring our faces. When he came with another vessel to throw into the well, I pointed my finger at him for the first time. It meant: Don't! Desist! I rejoiced, seeing that my finger had mastered an animal trainer's language.

Behind those red eyes, Father looked as though he would burst into tears. That did not deter me, and my finger continued to point. It continued to stay straight, not turning into a staring eye, a piece of abuse, or a double-barrelled gun. Like the erect penis of a soldier grinning at a prisoner, I kept it firm in Father's face.

The sadness that hung on Mother's eyelids grew heavier and heavier as the days passed. Father peed in bed some days. Shat right in the middle of the house. Mother cleaned it all up without a word. She sat up night after night at his bedside.

One morning, when Father was standing by the front door ready to pee, I grunted firmly. He jumped and turned to look at me. He then quickly retreated into his room, scared. That day, at noon, seeing Mother sneak out with something she was hiding, I raised my eyebrows at her to ask what it was. She knew Father's body language well, and so stopped and bowed her head. I asked again, my voice harsh. She opened her hands. It was his crap, wrapped in a yam leaf.

That night, I went to his room. Mother had fallen asleep, tired. He was not sleeping.

I ordered him with my eyes to come out. He came. I walked in front.

When we reached the fields that the railway tracks passed through, I turned and looked at him. The darkness had covered his head, like the black cloth on the face of a condemned man.

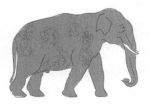

Leela

That evening, I'd been with Kunnel Pappan's son Joey who had been on a ship for two whole years. That's probably why I saw in my dream some goats, and people in woollen caps, and between them, Kalyaniamma who makes flower-garlands in the temple, all singing together on the high deck of a ship, which floated through a patch of rubber trees. I was asking the burly moustachioed fellow who stood at the ship's bow how on earth this oldie who couldn't even walk properly had clambered on board, when I heard someone knock on our door urgently.

Who the hell, this blasted night, muttered Padmini, as she leapt up from the bed, pulling her loose hair into a bun. She got to the door first, switching on the light before I could. I left behind the dream-travellers, groped around for my waist-cloth, tied it back on and followed her. The door was shaking as though it was having a fit; it was being pounded.

My wife snuck back behind me. Ask who it is, she whispered in my ear. I looked at her for a second, and raised my voice: 'Who's this?'

The rattling stopped.

'It's me.'

My wife went right back to bed muttering, oh it's old Kuttiyappan, God alone knows what twists and knots he's planned for tonight. I opened the door. There he was, shirtless, a towel wrapped around his head, a lungi around his waist, a six-battery torch in hand, and a huge smile on his face. I could not utter a word—he had grabbed my hand and pulled me out. As we went out, he dragging me on, I kept asking, what's up, Kuttiyappaa, but he kept walking briskly, pulling me after him. He paused only when we reached the rose-apple tree in the southern yard. I panted, leaning on its trunk. He hadn't let go of my hand.

'Pillecha,' he said to me, 'I need to fuck!'

'Who, me?' I asked. 'In the dead of night?'

'My dear Pillecha, this is no joke.' He scratched his back with the torch. 'This is a special kind of fuck. Need to make arrangements.'

'What on earth?' I was bemused.

He let go of my hand and was silent for a few minutes. Then he beamed the torch up the rose-apple tree.

'There's no one up there,' I assured him. 'Tell me.'

He could see that I was starting to lose my cool.

'Hey, how would it be to press a naked girl to the trunk of a tusker?'

I didn't say anything. He continued, 'Should look like its big golden nettippattom-ornament was taken off its forehead, left on the floor! Then I want her to stand on its trunk, holding on to its tusks.'

I inhaled sharply. A bat flew by suddenly, almost brushing against my forehead.

'Pillecha,' he called again in a low voice. I grunted.

'Why're you silent?'

'How'll this work, Kuttiyappaa?' My voice sank low with doubt.

'Oh, it will. Man goes looking for the moon. This is nothing like that,' he said. 'You just be with me!'

A bird screeched as it passed above our heads.

When I went back into the house after seeing him to the gate, my wife asked, 'What is it this time?'

'Oh, he wants to buy an elephant.' I fell into bed, facing away from Padmini.

'Some deadheads are born only to ruin what their fathers put together. He's got an education—what use?' she mumbled under her breath. I was mum. Just closed my eyes, hoping to get back to the ship of my dreams in the rubber tree-patch.

I went out only after my wife had left for work. I was about to step into Aniyan Pilla chettan's teashop when Kuttiyappan's Willys jeep braked right in front of me, and he commanded me to get in. I couldn't make out if it was him or his jeep that was snarling, but I climbed in. When we were past the junction, he said, 'There's a certain Elephant Soman Nair at Kidangoor. Let's catch hold of him for this trip!'

'Will he agree?'

'What's there to agree on?' His voice swooshed like a whistle. 'I'm paying hard cash!'

The jeep ran on as Kuttiyappan proceeded to tell me stories of elephants, their habits, and so on. In between, it (the jeep) began to talk, and I looked at Kuttiyappan with concern. No worries, he said. She's like that. Babbles sometimes. I left it at that.

When we reached Kidangoor, he asked me, 'Do you mind meeting with Elephant Soman Nair?'

'Not at all!'

'No, I meant I know that your wife's relatives live here … What if some distant relation … say from pissing together long ago … spots us …?'

That hadn't struck me. I thought for a moment and said, 'Just introduce me as someone else.'

There were more elephants than coconut trees in Soman Nair's yard. And at their feet, mounds of dung, like dried-up coconuts.

We waited for him for half an hour. He's doing his puja after his bath, his wife let us know. Eyeing a large tusker in the middle of the yard, Kuttiyappan asked, 'What about that one?'

I looked—and was afraid that his tusk would pierce right through my eye.

'How's he? They say he tore apart three mahouts.'

My insides shivered.

'What if he agrees to give it to us?' I asked.

'That's the fun! This Big Master will see what stuff we are made of!' Kuttiyappan said, looking at the strange slimy wet beast with lips between its limbs and no wings.

Soman Nair emerged after some time. His forehead was adorned with two lines of sandalwood-paste with an ochre zero in the middle. Seeing him, Kuttiyappan fell at his feet. Soman Nair had not expected that. I had, because this was Kuttiyappan. I stood by silently, watching the expressions flit on and off Soman Nair's face. Raising him up, Nair bade him sit. I too sat down. Kuttiyappan declined to sit and stood in a stooping salutation. Clearly, Soman Nair hadn't the foggiest; that much I could see.

'Why are you here', he asked.

Instead of answering that, Kuttiyappan started off with where we were from. I was cast as an elephant-lover from Thrissur who had recommended Soman Nair's elephants as the best in the land. Dear Lord Vasudevapurattappa, I prayed then and there, let this man ask me nothing! My tongue had been too closely ploughed by the Malayalam of Kottayam, and it was full of its rising and falling cadences; how was I to handle the taut, stretched sling-like ring of the north, of Thrissur? I was quiet as a mouse.

Luckily, Soman Nair did not ask me anything. Kuttiyappan was regaling him with everything under the sun about elephants, from elephant-ayurveda to *Mathangaleela*. Nair sat before him, his mouth open in admiration, and I just sat beside them, watching it all. In the end, Kuttiyappan took him aside and they conferred. Kuttiyappan fell at his feet again a few more times, as though he were a loose length of rope. Each time, Soman Nair's hands rose up on both sides like the venchamaram fans atop an elephant, swaying left and right, saying no, no …

Braking hard on the turn from Kidangoor to Pala, Kuttiyappan asked, 'What to do now?'

I just looked at him, throwing back the same question.

In between, the jeep growled. Kuttiyappan's ears grew keen. He turned to me. 'She says, go to the toddy shop there!'

I looked to the left; yes, there was one there, smiling at us.

Standing under the tiny strip of palm-thatch above the tiny shop in front of the toddy place, Kuttiyappan let out a burp that stank of fermented toddy.

'Pillecha, what if we go off to Bihar?' he asked.

I knew well he would do just that, so I said, 'Let's give it one more try, at Chambakkara?'

The shopkeeper craned his neck through the bunches of ripe bananas and asked, 'Are you here for a massage?'

'No, to buy an elephant.'

Curiosity came fully alive.

'For the temple procession?'

'No. Just to let it stand in front of my house.' Kuttiyappan spread lime on a betel-leaf.

'Alright, then speed away to Mannarkkad. A new fellow's been brought there—dark and shiny, like black rosewood! Our Rama Panikkar went there to take a look—he has all the right signs.'

'Rama Panikkar who?' Kuttiyappan could barely contain his anxiety.

'The first mahout of the famous Ettumanoor Neelakantan. His house is at the end of this lane. You can find out from him anything you like.'

Kuttiyappan and I threw glances at each other. The shopkeeper's head withdrew behind the bananas.

We went to Panikkar's house, taking with us a bottle of palm toddy, two packets of beedis and some betel-leaves and tobacco. He was at home, sitting on the veranda, holding an old lantern. They couldn't tell if he was tightening or loosening it. It was old and rusted, and looked like it was saying sadly—don't light me, the heat will be too much for my body. Standing in the yard, Kuttiyappan called out to him.

Panikkar put down the lantern and looked up.

'We're from Kudamaloor,' began Kuttiyappan, handing him all the gifts. 'Have seen Neelakantan ... You used to bring him to Karikulangara and Vasudevapuram, chetta.'

'Of course I did,' he agreed readily.

He wiped the dust from the half-wall on the veranda and bade us sit.

'Where in Kudamaloor?'

'I am from the south. This fellow's from another place. Koothattukulam.'

'South? Where in the south?'

'On the path that goes down from Pandavath, from Vattakkotta.'

Panikkar coughed and spat phlegm into the distance.

'It's the chill.' He coughed again, so hard his chest shook. 'Ediye ...' he called out then, and I followed his phlegm-choked voice, which entered the door and disappeared inside.

After some time, a woman came out with medicines and some water. Panikkar swallowed a couple of pills and handed her the glass. When Kuttiyappan's eyes went after her and then turned around to face him, Panikkar wiped his lips and said, 'Not my daughter. My wife. Everyone who comes here asks if she's my daughter. I'm telling you beforehand.'

Kuttiyappan laughed.

'I forgot that there was a girl at home, my first one, when I went here and there with the elephant.' Pannikar lit a beedi. 'One day, she left with a man. And after that, when I fell ill, I married this one. Need someone to take care of you, right?'

'My dear chetta, you know, my wife too left me like this one fine day.' Kuttiyappan looked as if he was about to burst into tears. 'I then married another. She left too.'

I let my gaze wander among the pictures of gods hung on the wall; they looked back at me. And then, we together looked at Kuttiyappan. He returned our gaze and then closed his eyes.

'Ayyo, that is sad, you young chap. What happened?' asked Panikkar, dragging his chair closer to him.

'My stars, what else!' Leaning towards Panikkar, he whispered in his ear, 'Chetta, to tell the truth, I have never known real sexual pleasure.'

Maybe Kuttiyappan's face made Panikkar feel sad for him. 'It will be alright,' he told him.

'It will be alright,' repeated Kuttiyappan.

He poured Panikkar a glass of toddy. When he felt its fervent touch on his tongue, Panikkar's eyes began to brighten up. When its whitish froth receded to the lees, Kuttiyappan made his first move. 'Chetta, we're here to ask you a favour.'

Panikkar wiped his face hard and looked at him.

'I want an elephant. For a day, or for just an hour.' His beseeching tone went and stood before Pannikar most humbly.

'What for?'

Kuttiyappan drained the last drops of toddy, making sure the dregs did not escape the bottle, and offered the answer along with the glass: 'To fuck a woman.'

Panikkar took another gulp and looked up.

'I want to make a girl stand on a tusker, and fuck her, pressing her back against its trunk.'

Panikkar drank up the rest in one gulp. The red spreading in his eyes surveyed Kuttiyappan.

'You'll get an elephant for a temple procession. Or to carry timber. Hard to find one for this,' Panikkar said, chewing the end of the beedi in his mouth.

Kuttiyappan sank down and sat at Pannikar's feet. Panikkar took a couple of puffs and told him, 'You are not going to find one anywhere around here. If you tell anyone, they'll thrash you with the elephant hook. There's just one way—go to Wayanad and meet Devassykkutty. He has an elephant.'

'Not just Wayanad, I'll go anywhere, to the other side of the earth. Please, please help me.' Kuttiyappan was pressing Panikkar's feet.

'He will agree if I tell him,' Panikkar said, with his eyes on the empty bottle. 'He came a long time back, looking for an elephant to finish off someone—his wife's lover. Waited for two days in the dark, but couldn't get him. He drops by when he comes this way. His present elephant, I chose. Anyway, try there. Tell him I sent you. Write down his address.'

Kuttiyappan wrote it down and saluted Panikkar once again with folded palms.

While stepping out, he told Panikkar, 'I paid for the bottle too, so don't pay for it when you go to the shop this evening.'

Panikkar coughed and nodded. A look flew out of the window and a head turned away sharply.

Kuttiyappan dropped me home in the evening. The daylight was now hurrying to get back into the sky. Padmini was in the veranda.

'So did it work, today's trip?'

'No, we'll have to go to Bihar.' My voice dipped.

'Since the dung has value, the money spent will be worth it!' She threw a searing look at me.

'My dear, don't say such things.' My voice fell even lower. 'It's a donation to the Kudamaloor church.'

'For what?' Her voice had grown arms and legs by now. 'To find a wife or to atone for all those sins?'

'What do you think he did?'

'Oh, don't get me started on that!' She killed the flame of the oil lamp with both hands and carried it inside. 'Elyamma chechi who cooks for him has been bedridden for two days; she fell down and badly injured her back. Where's he going to get rid of her curse, after making her fall? Good that his old man and woman are dead. Or they would have had to suffer too.'

I did not say a word in reply. I went straight into the bathroom, had a bath, combed my hair, and slapped some talc on my face.

'No point dousing yourself with all that talc after a bath; the stink of toddy stays!' Padmini's rage rose up along with the aroma of the food she was cooking. 'Drags others into shame too!'

I stared blankly at the ceiling.

I reluctantly mentioned the plan to go to Bihar as we were having dinner. Padmini kept eating as though she wasn't listening to me.

Kuttiyappan arrived in the morning. Hearing his jeep, she asked, 'So you are going to Bihar in a jeep?'

I did not reply; I had packed clothes for a week.

The light was now hurrying back to earth, and Kuttiyappan's vehicle cut right through it. The paperboy, Babu, who was coming from the opposite direction called out to him, and Kuttiyappan responded. When we reached the Chungam bridge, I asked him, 'Why did you break that Elyamma chettathy's back?'

Kuttiyappan turned his gaze towards the Meenachil River. 'Look, Pillecha, how it flows!'

I was mad at him now. 'Tell me why! Why did you hurt the poor woman?'

'My dear Pillecha, I didn't do a thing. Every day she comes up the steps to the room. Knocks on my door. Gives me black tea, and I drink it. If it went on like that every day, wouldn't it get boring? So I placed a ladder from the ground to my window and told her to climb up with the tea. Look, she's always picking pepper from the vines, and was *just fine* climbing up the ladder. She did have an accident the other day, but she's under excellent treatment. I told her to do it till her back is as good as new. She's on paid leave now. And even when she returns, she doesn't have to do any work, just be the chief chef, I've told her.'

'But that was really too much, Kuttiyappaa,' I could not help saying.

He stopped the jeep and relaxed in his seat.

'Not you too, Pillecha. Just think that it was her time to have a fall. I just kind of made way for it, putting that ladder there ...'

I had no words. He started the jeep, which kept babbling for some time without moving. Then it began to run, silently.

We reached the base-camp, and Kuttiyappan suggested we have a cup of tea before starting the climb. We stopped at a wayside teashop and also fed the jeep with a bottle of water. I had a momentary feeling that the cold wind was going to come down the mountain-pass and catch hold of my hand. There was no reason to feel that way. Nothing happened, though. As we climbed, Kuttiyappan said, 'I really want to die falling off this cliff. What about you?'

I craned my neck and looked into the gorge. It took some time for my eyes to reach deep down . When they came back, I said, 'Yes, me too—but what will Padmini think? Aren't we going now to Bihar?'

Kuttiyappan swerved expertly, missing a truck coming from the opposite direction by a whisker. 'God made that lorry miss its mark because he doesn't want Pillechan's wife to suffer.'

Suddenly, a Mysore-bound bus passed us, and we could see a kid thrust his head right out of its window. 'Good God,' said Kuttiyappan, 'that child is going to hit a post or something. Those assholes of parents aren't even looking,' he hollered. No one heard. The child's head kept bobbing outside the window like a balloon. The bus disappeared in the distance. Kuttiyappan stopped and started murmuring. It didn't sound like a prayer. Or maybe it did.

When we had crossed the mountain-pass, Kuttiyappan stopped near a man who was herding a cow and asked him where the elephant-owner Devassy's house was. The cow mooed at us and Kuttiyappan mooed back. And the cow smiled. Her owner said, 'It's near Ambalavayal. You have to turn from there.'

'Did you come here from Pala?' asked Kuttiyappan.

'My grandfather's from there, my grandmother's from Ranni,' he said, loosening the cow's tether. We bid the cow and her owner goodbye and set off for Ambalavayal. It wasn't hard to find Devassy's house. It was a huge structure located in the middle of a coffee-garden. The coffee had been harvested and laid out to dry in the sun. Two pairs of briefs and a vest hung on the clothesline to dry. A dog looked up hearing us and went back to whatever it was doing. There was no one else to be seen. Kuttiyappan tooted the horn a couple of times. After some time, an old woman opened a window and asked, 'Is it Thoma?'

'Yes, it is,' Kuttiyappan said, and I turned to look at him.

'What did the priest say?' She was staring through the bars of the window.

'He said, may you have good health and a long life, ammachi!'

The woman crossed herself and banged the window shut. I felt irritated. 'Couldn't you just ask her?'

Brushing off some dirt from his slippers with a coffee branch, he replied, 'Pillecha, no point asking her. From her face you can tell she is looking for Thoma. No point asking her about Devassy.'

I went up and knocked hard at her window. She opened it and asked again, 'Is it Thoma?'

'No, we are from Kottayam, we're looking for Devassykkutty. Is he here?'

The woman shut the window without a word. Kuttiyappan stared into the sky as if he hadn't seen that. I followed his gaze. What if Devassy was descending from the skies …

When a cuckoo started calling from a tree nearby, he said, 'Pillecha, long back, there were no cuckoos here. They've come here now that the summer has become really hot.'

The cuckoo flew away after some time. A leaf came falling down in a hurry to say something. The dog, which had been weighed down by deep thought all this time, now got up, shook its body, and took slow steps to the back of house. I plucked a couple of ripe coffee beans, put them in my mouth, and spat them out. Kuttiyappan then started telling the story of a slave. Not because I had asked. Maybe because he saw me putting the coffee beans in my mouth. This was the story:

Once, on a ship carrying coffee from Brazil, a slave who couldn't resist the aroma of the cargo became bold enough to sneak a taste of it. The captain punished him by stuffing coffee powder into every orifice of his body. Once he was dead, he took all the coffee powder out and distributed it to the other slaves. They were all delighted that they could finally have a taste of it; all except the littlest slave, who wept as he drank, for to him, it was the taste of his papa's death.

As Kuttiyappan told the story, I kept wondering where he managed to pick up such tales. I was still wondering when a small man showed up behind him. His arms were short, as though someone had pulled them up and tied them too close to each other on his shoulders. He looked at us both.

'From Kottayam,' said Kuttiyappan.

'Come this way,' he said.

We walked through the coffee garden after him.

'Is this Devassy?' I asked Kuttiyappan discreetly.

'Maybe. Maybe not. Never mind.'

The scent of coffee blooms pounced upon us intermittently, as we walked, like wild creatures. Every time that happened, I recalled the slave and his son, and shut my nostrils against it. Get thee away, I ordered, as though the scent were Satan himself. We finally reached a small hut screened off with palm thatch. Someone peered at us from inside. He brought a mat and laid it out. We sat on it. Kuttiyappan mentioned Panikkar. The small man nodded. He asked us what we were there for. Kuttiyappan told him. The small man remained silent, but wrote something in the air; Kuttiyappan seemed to be reading it. After he finished the air-scribbling, he said, 'Come to the southern edge of this garden tomorrow night, after ten. Or, on any day this week. But only after ten. With a hundred thousand rupees for an hour.' Kuttiyappan agreed.

We walked back through the coffee garden, the small man ahead of us. Once we reached the front of the house, he shook his head, bidding us farewell. Seeing the old lady opening the window and peering out, I asked him, 'Is that your mother?'

He did not look at me but at Kuttiyappan.

'Get in the jeep, Pillecha,' Kuttiyappan told me. I thought the scent of coffee was following us, so I told him to speed up.

We didn't stop anywhere; by the time it was dawn, we were in Kottayam. Kuttiyappan stopped in front of the Gandhi statue and bowed to both Gandhi and Lord Siva of the Tirunakkara temple next door.

'If I go home now I won't be able to get out again for sure,' I told him. 'Either we split now, or I find a room somewhere around here and hide for the time being.'

He let out a huge yawn and said, 'Let's get a room at Asoka Lodge, catch up on sleep, and then go to

Kumarakom. From there we'll collect the girl and drive back straight to Wayanad.'

I started at that suggestion. 'In this jeep?' I asked weakly.

'What's wrong with that? Our Usha will also be coming.'

So we got a room at Asoka. Kuttiyappan's snoring put up a mighty fight with the fan's grating sound as well as the din of the vehicles on the road. I tossed and turned.

It was past noon when we reached Kumarakom.

'You need a canoe to get to Usha's house. I can't swim,' I told him.

'Don't worry,' he said, 'if you die I'll bury you very respectably.'

'But aren't we in Bihar?' I asked him woefully. 'What will Padmini think?'

'In that case, I'll pray the hardest I can,' he promised. Before he finished, the canoe had steadied, and he splattered water on both sides with his hands, announcing triumphantly that God had heard our conversation. The boatman thrust the oar deeper.

When we had got off and were walking towards Usha's house, he suddenly turned around, grabbed me hard, and pointed towards a grassy thicket.

'Someone's crouching there!' He nearly chewed my ear like a rat. 'A bird! Cinnamon Bittern! The magician of the fields! You know, this is how the Vietnamese fucked the Americans back then, sneaking up from behind!'

I stared at his face, waiting for the deluge of historical facts. The thickets in front of us filled up with a pada-

pada-pada sound as the herons took flight together. He waved at them, and one of them waved back.

I asked, 'Are they from Vietnam?'

'No, hell, Pillecha, who could be from Vietnam here? Here everyone was for China-Russia bhai-bhai stuff, remember?'

As we walked on, we saw sliced tapioca laid out to dry in front of a house, and a torn red flag planted next to a floor mat. A few crows were enjoying a hearty meal there, not heeding the flag at all.

'You must be visiting Usha?' asked an old man.

Kuttiyappan pulled out the poet Vailoppilly's famous line to children—*you, who knows God himself, who can see beyond time*—to answer him. The old man couldn't make anything of it, but still suppressed a smile as he walked past us. I turned a few times to look at him; he was doing the same.

When we were some two or three coconut trees away from her house, Kuttiyappan started calling out to Usha. Well, hardly a house, to be fair. A roof of asbestos, palm-frond-thatch, and little else. Just an enclosure with walls of packing-case wood. The mud bund on which we were walking went round its back. A coop and some pots and pans were squatting there, wet from kitchen water. A cat sat there too, licking its paws. We could hear music, and angry voices blaring from a radio inside. Kuttiyappan called out to her again. The radio and the voices fell silent.

A woman sprang out from the kitchen side. Seeing him, her dark face almost bloomed.

'Oh my god,' she said blushing hard, 'look who's come!' Then, pausing a moment in joyful wonder, she said, 'Do come in, don't just stand there on the path.' The cat jumped in the way as she began to lead us inside, and she cursed and gave it a solid kick.

We sat on a mildly shivering bench.

'Saar, what would you like to drink? Coffee? Or, if we run now, we can get excellent evening toddy.' She was all ready.

'Nothing, Ushe, relax. Just relax,' he said, giving her a look that made her blush even more. Then he asked, 'Where's Damodaran?'

Not able to get over the blush, she said, 'Oh, he just went out. Must be in the toddy shop … or party office … where else will he go … You want to see him?'

'Oh no, was just asking,' said Kuttiyappan and then came straight to the point. 'Do you have some nice girl I can take to Wayanad for a day or two?'

The light disappeared from her face suddenly. 'My dear saar, there's two of them, but they work in a textile shop and have to get back home by evening, no matter what. That's the problem. They won't go anywhere far.'

Kuttiyappan rocked on the shivering bench and said, 'I need a nice young one for this.'

'Oh, I know your thing, oh don't I know!' Usha turned towards me. 'A long time back, he took me somewhere once, like this. I was new in the field then. He made me massage myself with oil all over, and then told me to dance to a song from a tape recorder! In my birthday suit! Ooh, I don't mind sleeping with ten men, but *that*, ooh! And after everything, just a kiss on the forehead!'

Kuttiyappan burst out laughing.

'So, what do we do now?' he asked, blowing the steam from the glass of coffee Usha had brought.

'Ask Das-appappy? Heard he's found some young ones,' Usha said.

Kuttiyappan sat there, blowing into the coffee. When we were about to leave, Usha gave us some fish curry in a plastic cover.

'*Vaala*-head curry. You can have it with the drinks.' I looked at her. It seemed that the kiss Kuttiyappan had planted on her forehead was still there.

She came with us some distance. Seeing the fields overgrown with weeds, I asked her, 'There's no farming done here anymore, is it?'

She replied, but to Kuttiyappan, 'Does this saar not read the papers?'

The chilli in Usha's fish curry seared my tongue even after we reached Kottayam. Kuttiyappan parked the jeep on the railway bridge, told me to stay inside, and went down somewhere through the small lines on the side. While I waited, two or three trains passed below, under the bridge. In between, someone came up and asked why I was there, and I told him, 'Just like that, no particular reason.'

'If you're here to get the stuff,' he said, 'the police is nosing around.'

He meant cannabis, but I didn't get him then, and was still thinking about it when Kuttiyappan hurried back inside and quickly started the jeep. The speed at which he drove, I was amazed this old thing could move so fast.

'The cops were at Das-appaappy's,' he told me. 'They took two kilos of stuff.'

Before he finished, we had reached the Tirunakkara ground.

'Not going there, I had fish,' I told him.

'Who's going in,' he said. 'Just look for Das-appaappy around there.' He pulled me by my hand and walked ahead. And as we were climbing the steps to the temple, we heard a song, like it was coming out of a cave:

> *Hear,*
> *O please hear,*
> *See,*
> *O please see,*
> *The crazy things some people do*
> *With leaves that in the forest grew*

It was Chatterjeemukherjee singing in the shade. He was originally from Vaikom, but had been here for a long time now. He had donated his only worldly possession, a Hindi dictionary, to Lord Siva of Tirunakkara. A long time back, during the Emergency, he had climbed the poovarashu tree near Anand Hotel and declared that he was the notorious Naxalite Vellathooval Stephen. The cough and body ache that the police had gifted him for that surfaced even now. From morning to evening, he would smoke, remembering the Lord of Kailas. He greeted Kuttiyappan with the beedi he was smoking.

'Shambho Mahadeva!' Kuttiyappan greeted him, taking the beedi. A puff of smoke climbed up and went somewhere. Chatterjee removed the waist-chain of the next beedi and started rubbing his palms to roll it.

Das-appaappy came down the steps after the evening prayers, puja-flowers stuffed behind his ears and pious streaks of sacred ash smeared all over his forehead. He hugged Kuttiyappan and said, 'Hey, just now only—ju... st now, I prayed, please let Kuttiyappan saar's life be a happy one.'

The stink of the fully rotten lie hit Kuttiyappan in the face, and he staggered a bit. The temple bull came to us. Kuttiyappan stroked its forehead. Don't let me disturb you, the bull seemed to say as it moved away. When it disappeared, Kuttiyappan asked, 'Any new stock?'

Das-appaappy turned towards the shrine and said, 'On my Lord-God, I swear—none. I could have got you Bindu, the one you had some time back. But she's gone off to the Gulf now to work as a nanny. She was so fond of you.'

He turned to me and said that he had set up Bindu first with Kuttiyappan. And Kuttiyappan had lain flat on the floor, covered like a corpse, with cottonwool in his ears and nose, and the lit oil lamp, sandal joss sticks and everything. 'You must wail and weep, he told her, like it's your own father lying dead. Oh, I still remember what she told me after—oh Das-appaappy, for some time, I just sat quiet, but when I kept looking, I began to feel what you'd feel towards a dad, and then I began to cry, and then I didn't know how to stop! After some time, he got up, wiped my tears, made me a hot coffee, and gave me lots of cash! ... Even now when she tells me this, she weeps.'

Kuttiyappan laughed out loud. So loud that some autorickshaw drivers on the road looked up, startled.

'What to do now?' Kuttiyappan asked.

Das-appaappy thought for a while and said, 'There's a chap from Arpookara in Kuttippuram. Been there for just a couple of months. He has a daughter. Sixteen. You may get her.'

'Oh, that would be the big bother,' said Kuttiyappan.

'No,' assured Das-appaappy. 'This fellow had made her pregnant once; it was our doctor who got rid of it. When people got wind of it, he scooted. I helped with selling the land. He's got plans to pimp her around, I think. You try.'

I began to feel a little afraid. I took Kuttiyappan aside and asked if we should do this. He threw me a look, and then went to Chatterjeemukherjee and got a puff and sang a line from *jo vaada kiya* ...

The Kuttippuram bridge looked like someone had been learning how to write the Malayalam alphabet 'na' on either side of it. As we crossed it, Kuttiyappan said, 'Just look who's lying below, with no clothes on at all!'

A huge body of sand lay stretched out under us.

'Oh, our Meenachil is so much better,' I quipped.

'Stop it, Pillecha,' he said. 'Don't stab a corpse.'

'Indeed, it'll swallow me up if I do!' I was angry.

'There's a saying up north—here—that if you see a snake and a migrant from the south—a chap like us—at the same time, kill the latter first! And look who's dead now? The river in the north! And did we kill it?'

The sand's breath came up to us.

We had some trouble finding the address. But after crossing a few people's backyards, we finally found Thankappan Nair's house. He sat inside, inhaling steam. Hearing us, he removed the mundu from his head. Bubbles of steam were stuck on his face like smallpox scars.

'Who?' he asked, his voice quivering slightly.

'We live nearby,' Kuttiyappan said.

Wiping his face, Thankappan Nair came out. The steamer kept making noises like someone muttering to themself.

'Das-appaappy from Kottayam told us to meet you,' Kuttiyappan told him.

Thankappan Nair's eyes gleamed with curiosity.

'Should we talk here', asked Kuttiyappan, 'or shall we go out?'

'I'll put on a shirt and be right back', he said, and walked briskly towards the house. His swollen testicles brushed against the white mulmul mundu.

I peeped inside the house a few times, but did not see anyone. Thankappan Nair came back wearing a shirt.

'How much is land worth here?' Kuttiyappan asked.

'Twelve', said Nair. 'The roof's leaking and the kitchen wall looks like it will fall any moment. Will need at least a lakh and a half to repair. But I have no cash.'

'Don't worry about cash. I'll give you two lakh outright. Ask if you want more.' Kuttiyappan put his arms around Nair's shoulder.

I looked at him then, and he asked, 'Tell me, Pillecha, isn't that the fair thing to do?'

I nodded. What else could I do?

Thankappan Nair climbed in behind us. 'Let's go for a ride', said Kuttiyappan.

After a while, he told Nair, 'Reach below the seat, and you'll find a bottle. Distilled by me! Give it a try.'

Nair hissed like a serpent as he downed cheekful after cheekful.

'How's it?

'Ambrosia, pure ambrosia!'

A sharp, seething smell filled the jeep.

Kuttiyappan stopped the jeep in a secluded place. When Nair started to get out, he walked over to his side and asked him to stay inside. All was quiet. I was so anxious, I thought the two would finish their lives standing quietly next to each other. Then Kuttiyappan broke the silence.

'You know why we're here, right?'

Nair nodded in agreement.

'But there's something more ...' Kuttiyappan said. 'Not sure how to put it, Nair chetta. I need your girl ... to press her against the trunk of an elephant and fuck ...'

How will a father take this, I thought, feeling my body burn. But Thankappan Nair was sticking out his tongue now and then as though he were seeking prey. He was actually mating the liquor's strength with the cold outside. He took another gulp and said, 'That's dangerous business; isn't it, saar?'

'What danger? It involves standing up instead of lying down. Against an elephant's trunk, instead of a wall, that's all!'

'But still ...' the father in him was doubtful.

Kuttiyappan continued: 'Don't we make little babies crawl under elephants? Don't we make them touch their trunks when they come bearing the temple deity? And for the elephant, it'll be just like an ant leaning.'

Nair was still shaking his head. Kuttiyappan pulled out a wad of notes and put it into his hands.

On the way back, Kuttiyappan asked to take a look at the girl.

'That's easy,' said the father. 'Aren't we going back to my place?'

Kuttiyappan said we would stay back in the jeep and he would bring her out. 'We can go out and get her some new clothes.'

When Nair left, I asked Kuttiyappan if this wasn't getting a bit too much.

He closed his eyes and said something under his breath, which didn't sound like a prayer, but maybe it was.

'Saar, here's my girl.'

I turned. A girl. Young and small, frail. I suddenly thought: Didn't my daughter look like her just some days back?

'Get in,' Kuttiyappan told her.

When we were driving, he asked, 'What's your name, molé?'

She did not reply

'My name is Kuttiyappan. This is Pillechan. He used to be in the Gulf. He came back and isn't doing much. I do nothing.'

The jeep hit a huge pothole on the road.

'You know, this Pillechan has a daughter just like you! Nice fair skin, big eyes ...'

For a second, my heart was weighed down totally.

'Tell me your name, molé,' he persisted.

'We call her ...' Nair began, but Kuttiyappan cut in and said, 'If she won't tell us, I am going to call her Leela.'

'That's a nice name,' said Nair, with a twisted smile.

I turned back to look at her. Her eyes had no light in them. Only the rise and fall of her chest indicated that she was alive.

In the textile shop, too, she was silent. Many colourful clothes fell on the table from the salesman's hands like birds that couldn't fly too high. I could see that she was oblivious of all this. Kuttiyappan called a salesgirl aside and told her to bring sets of lingerie, the ones with floral prints.

'What size?' she asked, blushing slightly.

'Oh, your size should be just fine,' he told her.

After the shopping, he asked her, 'Don't you want to eat something?'

'Yes, yes, I am famished.' It was Nair who replied.

Leela ate nothing; she just let her fingers wander on the food. The cold in them made the food go cold too.

'Eat, Leela,' Kuttiyappan tried to persuade her.

'Oh, don't mind her, saar,' said Nair. 'She doesn't eat much.' He was tearing the flesh from a bone. 'But let's get her mother a parcel.'

'Good husband!' Kuttiyappan exclaimed, putting an arm around his shoulders.

When we reached the lodge at Kuttippuram, I told Kuttiyappan, 'I am thinking of returning home tonight.'

'Now, that's unfair, Pillecha,' he protested, puffing hard on his cigarette. 'You want to cancel at the last minute?'

'That's not the thing,' I said, but did not know what more to say.

'Pillecha, I think I know. Now, why do you have to feel for that girl what her own dad doesn't feel? That's her fate! Even if someone else had approached him, Thankappan Nair would have done the same.'

'You won't understand, Kuttiyappa,' I said.

'Agreed. But don't go, please. Tomorrow night, after eleven, we'll jet back to Kottayam.'

I did not answer. He switched the lights off.

I could not sleep. The sound of vehicles kept coming into the room intermittently.

'Pillecha,' he spoke.

'What?'

'Tomorrow night, we are taking Leela back with us to Kottayam.'

'What madness!' I jumped up from bed.

'But why are you so scared? I am taking her to my house!' He laughed.

'What are people going to say?'

'What more can people say about me? They have nothing more left to say! Maybe that the oldster's brought a slip of a girl to live with him. Let them. But we can't leave her with her old man.'

'Then why not just leave with her tomorrow morning?'

'But won't the elephant be waiting for us in Wayanad? Devassy too? And am I not waiting for my wish to come to fruition? Let it happen, and then we can leave.'

'So what about the father?'

'Let's cut up his swollen testicles and feed them to the dogs.'

'Hey, easy!' I replied, really worried now.

'Don't worry, there's always a way out.'

In the dark, his snoring flew around my head like a bee's incessant hum. My eyes, which had by now adjusted to the darkness, turned towards him. His big tummy had got loose from his body and seemed ready to leap up and out. Unable to sleep, I watched it rise and fall.

When we drove through the mountain-pass into Wayanad, Kuttiyappan asked Leela, 'Heard of Archimedes' Principle?'

She did not reply.

'Know who fed poison to Socrates?'

She was still mum.

'Know which is the *Adikavyam*?'

I heard her father press his foot hard on hers and order, 'Speak, you ...'

I touched Kuttiyappan on the shoulder and said, 'No more.'

When we reached Devassy's house, Kuttiyappan and Nair got out and walked towards it. I stepped out too. A mild breeze was blowing.

'What is your real name, Leela?' I asked.

She did not speak, but looked at my face. An enormous sadness flowed from her eyes, I thought.

I moved away from the jeep. After a few minutes, I heard someone retch and turned around. Leela was vomiting, her head out of the jeep. I rubbed her back. When it was over, I fetched her some water. She washed her face with it and drank a little.

'That's because we came shaking inside this jeep all the way,' I said.

She threw me a look.

I could not return it.

After some time, Kuttiyappan and Nair returned. Devassy had asked them to come back at night. We reached Mananthawady, looking for a room in a lodge.

When dusk began to fall, Kuttiyappan told Nair that he could stay back in the room, and asked Leela to have a bath. We went to our room and bathed too. Before we went out, I told him that Leela had vomited. 'She isn't feeling well, I think.'

'Oh, that's alright,' he said, showering his armpits with scented talc. 'How's our Leela's new dress?'

I did not feel like saying anything.

As the jeep drew closer to Devassy's house, I turned to look. The dark seemed to ebb and eddy with the jeep's movement. In that dark, like a weak sliver of light: Leela.

We left the jeep in front of Devassy's house. The scent of coffee made me feel afraid again. In between, the old woman's window opened and closed once. It was dark inside there, too.

Devassy emerged suddenly from the dark. He took a look at Leela and said to us, 'Alright, you can walk this way,' and stepped into the coffee bushes.

We followed the light. I thought that the leaves of the bushes were brushing and nudging me like prostitutes. When we had gone some way, Devassy lifted his light a bit. The light caught two massive tusks. An elephant, as sombre as the night itself!

I was frightened.

'Pillecha, you stand in the shade of this teak tree,' Kuttiyappan suggested.

I nodded.

He called Leela and they went towards another tree.

The elephant's scent slowly spread all around me. My heartbeat ricocheted against the trunk of the tree.

'If you're done undressing, come over,' called Devassy to Kuttiyappan.

I saw Kuttiyappan and Leela walk naked towards the elephant. Devassy touched its trunk. So did Kuttiyappan. Then Devassy moved away. Kuttiyappan put his hands on Leela's shoulders and made her walk back slowly. Then he made her stand close to its trunk, between the tusks. He let go of her shoulders, moved back a few paces, and held the tusks fast with both hands. I looked at Leela. Did she know what her body was now pressing back against? The bristle-like skin on the trunk must already be hurting her frail body. The elephant's scent must be overpowering her.

The darkness seemed to be growing all around me like a huge tusker.

Kuttiyappan was going to take the first step towards the peak of his mad whim. My eyes stayed fixed on Leela, who stood between him and the elephant. I began to shiver from my toes upward. But his body did not move even a bit. It stayed opposite Leela's. He then took her hands in his. Releasing her slowly from the trunk, helping her move out from between the tusks, he kissed her tenderly on the forehead, like she was a tiny baby. Then he turned around and walked. Behind him walked Leela. Like a weird scene from some evolutionary past, there they were: a naked Kuttiyappan; behind him, a naked Leela; and behind them, the biggest animal on the earth.

Suddenly, Leela stopped and turned back. In a split second, a long arm extended towards her and held her close, then lifted her up and rubbed her against the sharp point of a tusk. It brought her down, laying her between its legs. And then the creature, the very personification of unfathomable darkness, lowered its weight on her, as if to fuck her.

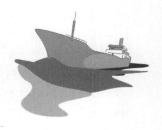

Badusha the Walker

Give me the ocean, the desert, or the wilderness!
Walking, Henry David Thoreau.

A key, a sea-shell, a leaf. These were the three things recovered from him. Because they suspected that a secret lay hidden in his grey hair, beard, mouth, or anus, they searched again. The seventy-year-old's naked body hung in the dim light of the tiny cell in the police station like a shadow.

'Look at the sonofabitch ...'

Smelling something he'd pulled out from between his teeth, the inspector spat.

'He don't care ...' added a policeman who stood near him.

The policemen, who came out of the cell, unable to extract anything from the man, looked glumly at the inspector. The inspector kept mining waste from between his teeth, sniffed at it pleasurably, and aimed his gaze at the man in the cell pointedly.

'What's he doing? Sleeping on his feet?'

A policeman stepped up and opened the door of the cell. The inspector went in and slapped the man hard on his cheeks.

'Medicine to wake you up,' said the policeman standing behind the inspector.

Stunned for a moment, the man looked at them helplessly. He then tried a slight smile.

'Nice smile!' said the inspector. The man looked at him gratefully. But in less than a second, the inspector grabbed his face, pushed him down violently, and shoved his elbow into his body. Then he stretched it straight and challenged, 'Okay, now smile.'

As the man tried to obey him, unable to plant his feet on the ground and straighten his twisted back, the inspector's fist landed on his nose and mouth. The blood that seeped down the corner of the man's mouth stained his fingers. He wiped it off on his victim's chest and said, 'Sonofabitch, I'll kill you.'

When he turned to leave, a voice walking on wobbly feet followed him—'Saar ...'

The inspector looked at him. He thought that some hideous creature stuck at some stage of evolution was calling out to him. He aimed a kick at the man's chest and asked, 'What is it, you pig?'

Gasping for breath, the man started to put together some words. The inspector grabbed him by his hair and hissed: 'Not a word out of you!'

He could neither see nor hear anything. The last spring of life within him was drying up.

'The fucking pig. Born liar!' cursed the inspector, as he came out of the cell.

'Saar, these fellows have special training probably,' said a policeman, handing him a note. The inspector nodded. 'The IG and the DGP will be here in an hour.'

The policemen looked at the inspector. 'Now we have to be here till this blasted thing gets over,' grumbled the inspector. 'Haven't had a wink of sleep.'

The clock struck four in the room, which stank of rotting coconut fibre.

The man in the cell tried to move a bit; a streak of pain shot straight through his spine like lightning.

Just three hours ago, he had stood under the sky on which moonlight lay sprawled. Before that, he had stood near Saufiya, who was leaning on the door of their house.

When he stepped out, she had asked, 'Aren't you crazy to be going for a walk in the dead of night?'

'Yes,' he had said.

'Don't you need a torch?'

He had pointed to the sky.

They had both smiled.

'Where are you walking to?'

'First to the beach ...'

'And then ...?'

'Inshallah.'

The houses were all fast asleep. Occasionally, a snore leaned out to peep into the road from one of them by the wayside. He stopped. When he went forward again, a dog leapt up in the yard of the house. It ran up to the gate, barking. He stopped again, fixed his eyes on its face, and introduced himself: 'My name is Badusha. What's yours?' Then he said, 'I'll call you Badu. That's what my father used to call me when I was a child.' The dog wagged its tail. 'Do you want to come with me for a walk?' It threw him a hesitant look, as if to ask, where to? Nowhere in particular, his eyes said. The dog fell silent. Maybe because it could not leave the house; the helplessness was evident on its face. 'Never mind, another time,' he said, and turned onto the road that went to the beach.

He dipped his toes in the surf. Raised his arms towards the sea. Touched the foreheads of the sleeping boats resting on the shore. Peed on the beach. Ran after the crabs.

A ship moved gently in the distance, rocking the milky layers of his cataracts. That belongs to the brother of Khoja Kassim, Baapa used to say. All the children would nod, looking beyond the finger he pointed. The ship was returning from a pilgrimage to Mecca, and Vasco da Gama set it on fire. All the women and children and men on it were burned to death. The children would then look sadly at Baapa's face. Tears would have welled up in his eyes by then. The envoy of the Sultan of Egypt, Javed Beg, was also on it. The children would nod. Now close your eyes. The children would obey. Do you hear the sound of the waves? Yes. Don't you hear the children wail? Yes. Now all of you may open your eyes. All eyes would open. All this while, Baapa would have been holding out his arm, pointing to the distance. On the other side, there was nothing but a dull, dirty wall.

Till the end of his life, Bappa lived in the past. Like a guard dog, barking memories. At the age of seventy, Badusha shut his eyes to detect the secrets his father had not told him. The waves sounded like prayers being recited. The solitude of the desert permeated the touch of the sand by the sea. When he opened his eyes, there were battleships, the scent of gunpowder, the screams of refugees and children. He sat down on the sand with the troubled mind of an old man living in a time in which memories had but short lives. An owl flew past him, sounding like an asthmatic.

He climbed back from the seashore and walked towards the island. From within the old godowns, pigeons cooed. The primitive signs of power—of the Dutch, the Portuguese, the British—lay everywhere.

The salty breeze touched his tattered cap and blew away.

At the corner where he was about to turn for the island, a police jeep braked just next to him.

'Where are you going?' It was the inspector who asked. He did not answer. Only glanced at him.

'Can't you hear?'

'I am just walking.'

'In the dead of night?'

'Yes.'

'What for?'

'I like to walk.'

'What's your name?'

'Badusha.'

The inspector looked at his men.

Badusha toppled from the unexpected blow delivered by the policeman standing behind him. They flung him like a ball into the back of their jeep, and held his head down with their feet.

It struck five at dawn.

The call to the *subahi* prayer reached the cell from which light had been debarred. It woke the man who stood leaning on the wall, eyes half-shut. Badusha touched his forehead, calloused from being pressed close to the earth for nearly seventy years, in prayer, to the floor that stank of piss and shit. As he pressed it again, in searing, simmering pain, 'How dare you! You fucking dirty pig! Are you trying to shit there squatting?' roared the inspector.

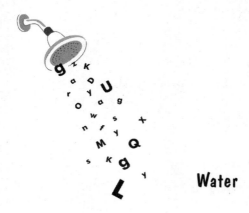

Water

The third day after W. G. Sebald passed away at the age of fifty-seven in a car accident, his driver died in another such accident. They found an obit about Sebald in his pocket. Just a few lines addressed to Professor. When the Professor stood with his arms crossed, you'd think he was the earth and its axes, both. Only when his old dog peeped out occasionally from under the old car in the workshop and withdrew could one spot a very reluctant smile emerge from behind his grey moustache.

During the funeral, the driver's children distributed the obit printed on cheap paper to the mourners.

Ashokan was sent this obit by a Capuchin monk from North Waltham who knew of his craze for obituaries. 'With the arrival of Sebald, my collection of obits hits five hundred,' he said, looking at the piece of paper no bigger than a man's palm. Chandran felt nothing, really; it was like looking at a cinema-notice. Chandran was Ashokan's assistant. Today his job was to dust and sort the obits in Ashokan's collection according to the year of appearance. At this time, Nandita and her friend Neena were in Radha's house for Nandita's research on the lives of widows.

'How old are you now, Radha?'

'Twenty-four?'

'When did your husband pass away?'

'Two years ago.'

'Children?'

'One. Three years old.'

'Do you work?'

'Yes, I got my husband's job when he died. I am a peon in a school.'

'Did you think of marrying again?'

'No.'

'Why?'

'Just didn't think of it. Right now I want to raise my kid well.'

'That's what every mother would wish. But don't we women have other desires too?'

'I'll pray to the Goddess, to be spared such desires.'

'But aren't those desires natural?'

'Please don't ask me such questions. Talk about something else …?'

Nandita and Neena looked at each other, trying to figure out what to ask Radha next. At this time, Chandran was examining a somewhat torn piece of paper, turning it over. 'It's in French,' said Ashokan. 'An obit written for Gérard de Nerval by Danny Boone, an opium-seller, in the pages of *Revue de Paris*.' Ashokan took it from him and tried to stick together the torn pieces. The opening line that began with the phrase 'On the streets of Paris ...' would not stick and so stayed apart from the rest. One could begin reading the orbit only from the line that said that Nerval walking Tibu the sea-crab, holding on to its blue silken leash, was a common sight. Nerval believed that crabs were harmless, peaceful and serious creatures. So he had a special fondness for them. They did not bark like dogs. They did not take over anyone's private life. Once, when I went to meet Nerval with opium, I found him running around screaming in his room, stark naked. His face trembling, he told me that he could not finish his poem. I handed him the opium. He squatted on the chair behind his desk and pressed the opium between his teeth. The bitterness made him frown slightly. Then he picked up Tibu and went to the desk. He dipped its feet in ink and sent it walking on paper. The strange shapes that emerged from the crab's feet, he read them like they were a familiar script. Then he went on to finish the poem triumphantly. In that moment, I began to doubt who he really was, and ran out of the room.

By the time he finished reading this note, Ashokan, too, was squatting on the chair behind his desk, naked. When Chandran looked at him from a corner of the room, Nandita and Neena were at Elizabeth's house.

'How many years ago did he pass away?'

'Fifteen, next month.'

'Who else lives here?'

'My in-laws, three cows, four goats and two fowls.'

'What did your husband do?'

'He farmed. Went down with chest pain one day.'

'Who runs it all now?'

'The farm belongs to his brothers. The house isn't partitioned yet. I take care of it all by myself.'

'Didn't you ever feel like marrying a second time?'

'It's not enough to feel it, is it? I went back to my parents for some time after his funeral. The day I came back, Appan and Amma made me lie down at night on a mat by their door. I just have to make sure that I am up and away before they get up. Else it would be a bad omen!'

'Children?'

'They all thought I was barren. But actually he couldn't … what's the point in saying this now? He's dead and gone, the poor man.'

When Nandita and Neena stepped out of Elizabeth's house, Ashokan was still sitting the same way.

They came out of Kajuthumma's house just when Chandran was done rearranging the second rack.

'Kajuthumma and Ashokan's mother are the same age. Umma looks a hundred at least—Ashokan's mother can pass off as his sister, his friends say.'

'Isn't she a widow?'

'Yes, widowed at seventeen. A month after Ashokan was born. Would you believe it? She does yoga and keeps her body shipshape.'

'She must surely be in a relationship, then.'

'I have asked Ashokan many times. He gives me the slip every time.'

'Have you not met her yet?'

'No. I have told him I want to. But he won't budge.'

'Some women are envious of their daughters-in-law. Especially those who are widowed early.'

'But I am not that, uh … just his live-in partner.'

'Someone who puts up with all his crazy ways!'

'Right you are. He's as obsessed with water as with obits. Sex has to be either in the bathtub or under the shower!'

'He can't have it dry, is it? Has to be wet?'

'Yeah. He says a dry body is a dead one. The water flowing down a bare body isn't water—it is the body itself. Let's flow together, that's what he says.'

When Nandita returned to the apartment, Chandran had changed out of his work-mundu, the day's work done. She did not wait for the lift and walked up five floors. The door wasn't locked. Seeing Ashokan sitting naked on the chair, she asked him if he had been born just then, or in the morning itself. Ashokan, who would have normally smiled and replied, told her, 'Go have a bath and a coffee if you are tired.' When Nandita hesitated, noting the unusually sombre mood, he said, 'They called from home. Mother's dead.'

Ashokan was driving, as usual, very slowly, very carefully. The silence between them was so fragile, it could collapse any moment. Then he himself evacuated it, boasting mildly that he possessed an obit of the French painter Theophile Kraus, by a woman called Emma Greene, in her own hand.

Theophile Kraus had learned of his mother's death and was walking to his house miles away in the night when he passed by the open window of a brothel, and heard a girl recite Verlaine's poetry. He went in. The girl who was reciting the poem was very plain, entirely unattractive. He told her to recite other poems of Verlaine. For three whole days, he listened to her recitation. By then, he had forgotten that his mother had passed away. Theophile Kraus died banging his head on the walls of a mental asylum. Emma Greene was the woman who brought him food there every day. Finishing the story, Ashokan asked Nandita, 'Isn't Verlaine's "Savithri" a great poem?'

When they reached, Nandita noticed that people were looking at her; she was, after all, much younger than Ashokan. Even when they were speaking to him, their restless eyes sought her. 'She's been laid inside,' an older woman said. Ashokan did not reply. 'We've put two benches in the room. She can be bathed there, I've told your aunts. And then we can shift her to the veranda,' said a man who looked like a family elder.

Ashokan and Nandita stepped into the room where she lay. She was wearing a light blue saree. In the fit of envy that bubbled up inside her at the sight of her beautiful face, for a moment, Nandita forgot that it was a corpse. 'So let's bathe her,' said the elderly man. Ashokan nodded, then lowered his voice, asking everyone to leave. They were now alone beside her. 'Don't stand here, Nandita,' Ashokan said. 'I'll bathe her alone.' She stood there for a few more minutes and then stepped out. She heard the door being bolted. As she stood outside, leaning on the wall behind her, the water began to gurgle inside.

Translator's Note

Unni R. represents a new generation of male short story writers who have, perhaps for the very first time in the history of Malayalam literature, chosen to turn a searing eye on what is too often deemed as the very grounds of literary creativity in Malayalam: the Malayali macho masculine. In Kerala, especially in instances of moral policing (very frequent, and now fiercely opposed by people of other genders, and many men too), one comes across references to *nattukaar*, or 'local people', as its agents. This innocuous-sounding reference conceals a vicious form of masculine power—groups of men of particular localities who monopolise public spaces and violently suppress any sign of subversion or opposition by women and others. Unni and some other contemporaries examine the psychology of this highly homosocial group; Unni, especially, from the inside.

He carefully lays it all out in front of his readers' eyes. For example, the chief protagonist of 'Leela', Kuttiyappan, is rich, independent, free from all the constraints of a householder, intensely narcissistic and amoral, hence prone to using all the people around him for his ends, cruel and playful at the same time. The macho man's homosociality, as depicted in 'Holiday Fun', is inherently feudal and violent, and soon unravels into deadly assault on the less violent. The 'small man' who is often Unni's narrator, is often a meek and ineffective husband who lives off his wife's hard labour and is willing to suffer her ennui. It is often through their eyes that readers get to see the deflation and downfall of the macho man. But 'small men' are only one shade in a whole spectrum of the masculine that Unni unveils. Indeed, this spectrum shades into the feminine—notice Jesus in 'He Who Went Alone'. Unni also powerfully pursues those who are excluded and victimised by elite masculinity. For such behaviour is not merely gendered, but shaped by caste privilege as well. Those who resist are diverse: lesbians, gay men, dalit workers. The playfulness, aggression and performance of women in his stories are indeed very different from that of the macho male.

Unni's stories are all set in a real place, the (now peri-urban) village of Kudamalloor in the Kottayam district of Kerala, his home-village. It is sociologically diverse, with people of different faiths living together in close proximity. For a translator, the challenge is to capture the relaxed, laid-back pace of life in a place shaped as powerfully by nature's rhythms as by the routines of human life, and the multiple layers of his Malayalam, which are sometimes crucial to the story's denouement itself. Also, his storytelling tends to mirror the sociological richness of the place it refers to, with the Hindu epics, the Bible, local historical memory and lore, and Malayalam literature itself forming layers, or twisting themselves in discernable strands. Some of his stories also strongly allude to well-known texts and figures in Malayalam literature; 'Householder' is about one of them—Vailoppilly Sreedhara Menon, one of Malayalam's most beloved poets of all times, an incorrigible loner who could allegedly converse with crows. Retaining each of these layers with care and precision has been the second key challenge, and I have enjoyed it thoroughly.

I thank Unni for inviting me to translate his work and Minakshi Thakur for offering to publish my work, for her excellent editorial suggestions, and her patience.